LISTEN WITH MOTHER

LISTEN
WITH MOTHER

Illustrated by Priscilla Lamont

*Published in association
with the BBC*

HUTCHINSON
London Melbourne Sydney Auckland Johannesburg

Hutchinson & Co. (Publishers) Ltd
An imprint of the Hutchinson Publishing Group
17–21 Conway Street, London W1P 5HL

Hutchinson Group (Australia) Pty Ltd
30–32 Cremorne Street, Richmond South, Victoria 3121
PO Box 151, Broadway, New South Wales 2007

Hutchinson Group (NZ) Ltd
32–34 View Road, PO Box 40-086, Glenfield, Auckland 10

Hutchinson Group (SA) (Pty) Ltd
PO Box 337, Bergvlei 2012, South Africa

First published 1982
Set in Baskerville by Bookens, Saffron Walden

Printed in Great Britain by The Anchor Press Ltd
and bound by Wm Brendon & Son Ltd,
both of Tiptree, Essex

ISBN 0 09 147160 5

Contents

Preface

I've always liked telling stories. When I was at boarding-school I used to frighten the wits out of the girls in the 'dorm', telling gruesome ghost stories when the lights were out!

I love reading stories on the radio – for grown-ups and children. But best of all, I like reading to my own children. Ben is seven now and can read for himself but he still loves snuggling up and being read to. (He would die if he knew I'd told you that.) Mari-Claire is two and a half and a live Jumping Bean from about 6 a.m. to 7 p.m., when she reluctantly agrees to leave the action and go to bed. But for about ten minutes she will sit *completely* still if I read to her.

What I mean is, reading stories is so much more than the act of speaking out loud the printed page; it's an involvement with each other as a little unit – parent and child – a shared and imaginative experience. This is why 'Listen with Mother' is such a comforting *timeless* phrase and why the programme is so durable. I listened to it with my Mum, and Mari-Claire listens to it with me.

And I love taking part in it – it's a joy!

Some of the best stories are in this book. So, for the Jumping Bean and thousands of children everywhere, are you sitting comfortably? Then I'll begin.

Nerys Hughes

The night Dad brought home a pig

Judith Drazin

Are you sitting comfortably? Then I'll begin.

'Where's our Dad gone?' said Joey.

'Where's our Dad gone?' said Lynne.

'Bother the man,' said Mum, 'he's gone to the fair to win a pig.'

That night Dad came home with a pink pig under one arm.

'Bother the man,' said Mum, 'where can we put a pig in a high-up flat?'

The pig spent the night in the downstairs laundry. He tramped over Grandpa's clean shirts and he tried to eat Mum's best blue pillow case.

11

'Bother the pig,' said Mum, 'take it away and bring back something else.'

'All right, all right, all right,' said Dad, 'I will go out and do a swop.'

'I wonder what Dad will bring,' said Joey.

'I wonder what Dad will bring,' said Lynne.

That night Dad came home with a statue. It was a lady with a long dress and long hair.

'Bother the man,' said Mum, 'where can a statue go without a garden?'

In the end they put the statue on the balcony. She got all tangled up with Mum's washing line.

'All right, all right, all right,' said Dad, 'I will go out and do a swop.'

'What will he bring home next?' said Joey.

'What will he bring home next?' said Lynne.

That night there was a terrible noise on the stairs. Dad was bringing home a piano with his friend from along the street.

'Now we can all have a bit of music,' said Dad.

'Bother the man,' said Mum, 'that piano is much too big to get through the door.'

The piano spent the night on the landing. Grandpa bumped into it on his way upstairs and was very cross.

'All right, all right, all right,' said Dad, 'I am just going out to do a swop.'

Dad went out for a long, long time. That night he came home with nothing under his arm.

12

'Why didn't you bring anything?' said Joey.

'Why didn't you bring anything?' said Lynne.

Dad gave a big smile. 'How would you like to go on a trip?' he said. 'How would you like to go on a trip to the seaside?'

'Can I have ice-cream?' said Joey.

'Can I go paddling all day long?' said Lynne.

'Can I sit in a deckchair and put my feet up?' said Mum.

'That's right,' said Dad, 'I swopped the pig for a statue and I swopped the statue for a piano and I swopped the piano for a trip to the seaside. Now Lynne can go paddling and Joey can eat ice-cream and Mum can sit in a deckchair with her feet up.'

'Good old Dad,' said Joey.

'Good old Dad,' said Lynne.

'Why, bless the man,' said Mum, 'it's just what I wanted.'

And off she went to make a cup of tea.

Fishfingers and custard

Jane Holiday

Are you sitting comfortably? Then I'll begin.

'What do you want for your dinner, love?' Sharon's Mum asked her.

'I'm just having an apple and a banana but *you* must have something cooked.'

'Mm . . . .' Sharon thought for a moment. 'Fishfingers please,' she said at last, 'and . . . custard.'

'*Fishfingers* and *custard*?' said her Mum. 'Fishfingers and custard? You can't have that.'

'Why not?' Sharon asked grumpily. 'Why can't I? You asked me! You asked me what I wanted.'

'You can't have it,' said her mother, 'because you *don't* eat fishfingers with custard. You can have fishfingers and chips though, and some nice green peas.'

Sharon was cross.

She covered all the fishfingers and all the chips and all the peas with tomato ketchup.

Then she cut it all up into teeny tiny pieces.

Then she put salt and pepper on it.

Then she ate it – as *slowly* as she possibly could.

Sharon's Mum sighed. 'Do eat up Sharon,' she said. 'It'll get cold.'

'Don't care,' said Sharon, but she ate it up at last because she *was* hungry.

Next day Sharon's Dad cooked her dinner.

'What do you want for dinner, Sharon?' asked Dad. 'I'm just having a cheese sandwich but you ought to have something cooked.'

'Fishfingers and custard please,' said Sharon, quick as a flash.

'No you don't!' laughed Dad. 'You had fishfingers yesterday, didn't you? I'll cook you some sausage and mash.'

Sharon was cross.

She covered all the sausages and all the mashed potato with tomato ketchup. Then she cut it all up into teeny tiny pieces.

Sharon's Dad sighed.

'Eat up Sharon,' he said. 'I cook a lovely meal and you just mess it about.'

Sharon scowled, but she ate it up at last because she was hungry.

The next day Sharon went to see Granny and had dinner with her.

'Now what would you like for dinner, Sharon?' Gran asked her. 'I'm having a boiled egg because I don't eat much.'

'Can I have whatever I like?' asked Sharon.

'Yes,' said Granny, 'as long as I've got it in the house.'

'Then I want *fishfingers* and *custard*,' said Sharon. 'That's what I want, please, Granny.'

'Right,' said Granny. 'Pass my little milk-saucepan dear, will you?'

In a few minutes they sat down to eat.

In front of Granny was a lovely brown egg in an eggcup, with bread and butter on a plate beside it.

In Sharon's place was a plate with three fishfingers on it. Next to it on a little mat stood a small jug.

'Help yourself to custard dear,' Granny said calmly, tapping her egg with a spoon.

Sharon poured the thick yellow custard over her fishfingers. 'At last,' she thought.

'What did you have for dinner?' Mum and Dad asked her that evening when she was back home.

'Fishfingers and custard,' said Sharon.

'Oh!' said Mum, sounding a bit cross.

'Oh!' said Dad. He didn't sound very pleased either.

'It was *horrible*,' said Sharon. 'But I ate it all up because Granny made it *specially*.'

'You little fusspot!' laughed Dad. 'You keep on asking for fishfingers and custard and when you get it, you don't like it!'

'You're a big silly,' said Mum.

'So what do you want to eat for dinner tomorrow then?' asked Dad.

'I know *just* what I want!' said Sharon. 'Something *really* nice!'

'What?' asked Mum and Dad.

'SAUSAGES and RASPBERRY JAM,' said Sharon.

'Oh . . . Sharon!' said her Mum. 'You're *impossible*!'

The flying rabbit

Kenneth McLeish

Are you sitting comfortably? Then I'll begin.

One day, Small Rabbit was out in the meadow, as usual. He looked up at the birds in the sky. He thought to himself, 'I'm tired of walking about on the ground all the time. I'm going to fly, like the birds.'

He climbed a tree. It wasn't easy, because his front legs were too short and his back legs were too long.

When he was half way up, he looked down. The ground was a long way off. 'All right,' he thought. 'Now's the time to fly!'

18

He spread his front legs out like wings, and gave a great big rabbit-jump off his branch.

But he was lucky, for just underneath his flying-branch was the nest of the Crow family. He landed in it with a bump.

'Ow!' said the two little crows. 'Watch where you're falling!'

Small Rabbit didn't answer. He was wondering why he hadn't been able to fly. 'Can you fly?' he asked the little crows.

'Not yet,' they answered. 'But we will one day, if we try hard enough.'

'So will I,' said Small Rabbit. 'I'll stay here with you until then.'

Small Rabbit stayed in the Crows' nest all day. It was a bit of a squeeze, especially when Mr and Mrs Crow came back. They weren't pleased to find a new rabbit baby in their nest.

As it began to get dark, Mrs Rabbit noticed that Small was missing. She went out to the edge of the field to look for him. 'Small?' she called. 'Sma-all! Where are you?'

'Up here,' said Small, poking his head over the side of the Crows' nest.

'Good gracious! Whatever are you doing up there?' asked Mrs Rabbit.

'Learning to fly.'

'Come down, you silly child. Rabbits don't fly.'

'I won't come down.'

19

His mother went back to the burrow and fetched Mr Rabbit. He came and sat beside her under the tree. 'Be careful, Small,' he said. 'It's a long way down.'

All the nine little rabbits came too. They all sat in a row under the tree, looking up at Small.

No one knew what to do. Mr and Mrs Crow began to get cross. 'Look,' they said to Small. 'you can't stay here all night. There isn't room.'

'It won't take all night,' answered Small. 'As soon as I can fly, I'll go.'

'But rabbits can't fly,' shouted the Crows.

'In that case, I'll make rabbit history,' answered Small.

The Crows got angrier and angrier. The two baby crows were squashed under Small's furry tail. The big crows had to sit hanging over the edge of the nest. They looked like umbrellas that hadn't been folded up properly.

At last Mr Crow lost his temper. 'You stay here,' he said to Mrs Crow. 'I'm going out.' And off he flew.

So there they all sat, eleven rabbits in the field under the tree, and one rabbit and three crows in the nest. The biggest crow was hanging over the edge. The shadows of night began to creep across the field.

Mr Crow was away a long time. At last, just as the sun was beginning to disappear behind the hills, he came flying back. He landed on the side of the nest, and nearly fell off again, there was so little room.

'It's all right,' he said. 'I've been to see Owl and he's told me what to do.'

'What did he say?' asked Mrs Crow.

'Come up here and I'll tell you,' answered Mr Crow.

Mr and Mrs Crow flew to a branch higher up the tree, and he whispered into her ear behind his wing. No one else said anything. The eleven rabbits in the field, and the one rabbit and two crows in the nest, sat still and waited.

At last Mr and Mrs Crow came back. 'Come on, little crows,' said Mr Crow. 'Time to be going.'

'Going? Going where?' said the little crows.

'To the rabbit warren, of course. If rabbits are going to start flying, crows will have to start living in holes in the ground. Down we go!'

He picked up one of the little crows in his beak, and flew off. Mrs Crow elbowed Small out of the way with her wing, and flew off with the other little crow. They circled round and down, towards the rabbit burrow on the other side of the field.

Small watched them go. All at once he began to feel lonely. The sun had almost gone. He was getting cold, all on his own in the nest. He looked down. The eleven rabbits from his family were still sitting on the ground watching him.

'I . . . I think I'd better come down,' he said.

'All right,' said Mr Rabbit. 'Are you going to fly?'

'Not today. I don't feel much like flying any more. Rabbits ought to stay on the ground, and leave flying to the birds.'

'How will you get down then?'

'I'll have to jump,' said Small nervously. 'Will you catch me?'

'You can't jump,' his mother said. 'You'll hurt yourself.'

'I know,' said Mr Rabbit suddenly. He whispered to the other rabbits. Then he and Mrs Rabbit lay down, and Large climbed on to their backs. When he was ready the Medium Twins climbed up and balanced on top of his head. Then the bravest of the Triplets climbed up and stood on their heads. Soon there was a ladder of rabbits, reaching all the way up to the Crows' nest. The baby rabbits were too small to climb, but they stood by ready to catch anyone who fell.

'Come on, Small,' said Mr Rabbit in a squashed sort of voice. 'Be quick, before we all fall over.'

As soon as Small was down, the rabbit ladder unsorted itself.

'Thank goodness for that,' said Mr Rabbit. 'It was flat work being at the bottom.'

'Don't ever do a thing like that again,' said Mrs Rabbit crossly to Small. 'Look what's happened now. We've got a family of Crows moved into our burrow. How are we going to get rid of them?'

But there was no need. As soon as the Crow family saw that their nest was empty, they flew back and put the baby crows safely inside it. 'We'll move into a new one tomorrow. As high as we can go,' said Mr Crow.

That's why, if you go and look, you'll find that all crows live in nests right at the top of very high trees. And rabbits stay on the ground.

The crotchety tooth

Margaret Hopkins

Are you sitting comfortably? Then I'll begin.

Once there were two rows of happy little teeth. One row was up at the top of the mouth, the other row was down at the bottom, and they worked together every mealtime chewing meat and peas and sausages and apple tart. Sometimes there was jelly, which was easy because they didn't have to bite that. Sometimes there were crisps, and they did enjoy making a crunchy crackly sound as they munched away at them. And sometimes there were sweets, and then they could crunch them up quickly if they liked, or, if they felt tired, they could leave them alone and make them last a long time.

So all day long the teeth were kept busy. The little sharp ones at the front would bite off the food, and the wide knobbly ones at the back would chew it up into small pieces. And at night the upper row cuddled down next to the lower one, and they all went quietly to sleep.

24

Then one morning at breakfast something strange happened. The little teeth were busy with a boiled egg and bread and butter fingers, when one of the bottom front teeth said, 'Ow! That piece of crust hurt!'

'Don't be silly,' said his twin brother next to him, 'crusts can't hurt.'

'Well that one did,' said the first tooth crossly. 'Ow! So did that. I'm not going to bite anything more this breakfast time. Let the teeth round the corner do it all.'

So for the rest of that meal the food had to come in sideways so that the other teeth could bite it.

Then again at dinner time the crotchety tooth said, 'Ow! That piece of potato hurt!'

'Don't be silly,' said his twin again, 'potatoes can't hurt.'

'That one did,' said the crotchety tooth, and once again he refused to bite anything more.

This went on for two days. Then one evening when they were settling down to sleep, one of the top teeth, the one who liked to cuddle up against the crotchety tooth, suddenly said to him, 'Keep still, can't you? You're wiggling around and keeping me awake.'

'I want to wiggle,' said the crotchety tooth. 'I want to wiggle and wiggle.'

'Don't be silly,' said his twin sleepily, 'teeth

can't wiggle.'

'But I can!' the crotchety tooth cried out. 'Just feel me then!' And he moved backwards and forwards so much that the teeth on either side of him could feel that he certainly was loose.

'Stop it,' said his friend from above. 'How can we sleep with you doing that?'

'I don't care!' he giggled. 'I'm clever! I can do what you can't do. I can wiggle like this, and this. Ow! It hurt that time. All right, I won't move any more tonight.'

He went to sleep soon after that, tired out by all his wiggling. But the other teeth stayed awake for a long time, whispering about him.

'I can't understand it,' said the one from the top row. 'Teeth don't move. Teeth can't move. But he did. It's very strange.'

And it grew stranger. After two more days even the teeth right at the very back could see that the crotchety tooth could wiggle so much that sometimes he seemed to be lying right down.

And he did no work at all. He wouldn't let food come anywhere near him. This meant that the teeth near him couldn't do anything either, and the back teeth were getting tired out with all the extra work they had to do.

Then came the strangest thing of all.

It was evening, and the teeth had had their scrub and were ready for bed when some of the front teeth saw that there was an apple coming. Now they were bored with doing nothing all day, so before the crotchety tooth could say 'no' they took a big bite.

'*Owwww!*' screamed the crotchety tooth. 'That's not fair! I didn't want to bite! And I won't bite ever again! I'm going to jump out and leave you all.'

With that he hopped out of his place and never came back again. What happened to him then? The other teeth never knew for sure. They did see him being put under the pillow, but next morning when the pillow was lifted up they saw that he had gone, quite gone. There was some shiny money there, but no tooth.

They had to start breakfast with one biter missing. This wasn't too bad, they found, in fact it was easier than it had been the day before, because at least the rest of the front teeth were allowed to do their proper work. But they found it hard to bite together properly and this worried them.

'How can we manage with a big gap like this?' asked one of them. 'We need a tooth in that space.'

'Please, Sir,' squeaked a little voice, 'please, Sir. I'm growing as quickly as I can.'

'Who said that?' asked another one.

'Please sir,' came the squeaky voice again,

'please, I'm the new tooth. I'm growing in the gap.'

The teeth looked down into the gap and there, sure enough, was the tiny white tip of a new tooth coming up.

'How did you get there?' gasped all the teeth.

'I grew!' said the little one proudly. 'I've been growing for several days. I was trying to push that old tooth out. He was sitting on my head!'

'You poor dear thing,' said the others kindly.

'Well, you're as bad,' the new one replied indignantly. 'Some of you are sitting on top of my baby brothers. They're going to start pushing you out soon. You just wait and see. You'll be put under the pillow too.'

The other teeth all cried, 'Nonsense!' They thought that the new tooth was making it all up. He seemed too sweet to want to push them out. But the crotchety tooth's twin had been lonely since his brother had left, and he thought to himself, 'I think the new tooth is right. I think his brothers will push us out, but I don't mind leaving. I want to find my twin. I'd like to see what happens under the pillow and how the money gets there. I hope it will be my turn soon. Now I come to think of it, that crust at breakfast did hurt a bit.'

And so he looked forward to the time when he too would be loose enough to come out and go under the pillow.

The hippo who tried to catch cold

Daphne Lister

Are you sitting comfortably? Then I'll begin.

Once there was a small hippopotamus who wanted a handkerchief. He wanted one more than anything else in the world.

He asked his mother for one, but she said, 'Don't be silly! You haven't got a cold.'

Little Hippo thought about this for a while.

'Well,' he said to himself, 'I had better try and catch a cold and then maybe I can have a handkerchief.'

But he didn't know how to catch a cold, so he went to the park to think about it and lay down on the grass and soon he fell fast asleep. When he woke up some people were standing staring at him.

'I shouldn't lie there if I were you,' said an old lady kindly. 'The grass is damp and you might catch cold.'

'Goody!' said Little Hippo.

'What's good about catching cold?' said Tom the Postman, scratching his head.

'Well, then I can have a handkerchief,' explained Little Hippo.

Some children laughed. 'You don't need a cold to have a handkerchief,' said a little boy called Michael.

'*I* do,' said Little Hippo sadly. 'My mother can't think of any other reason to have one. Can you?'

'You *might* need one to collect conkers in,' suggested Michael, and he took a green handkerchief out of his pocket and held the corners together so that it made a little bag.

'Or to make a sunhat on a very hot day,' said Tom the Postman, taking out a big checked handkerchief and knotting the corners. Then he took off his postman's cap and put on the handkerchief sunhat.

'Or to bandage your foot if you had an accident,' said Sue the Nurse, and she folded her very clean white handkerchief to make a bandage.

'Or to dry your eyes if you hear a sad story and it makes you cry a little bit,' said the old lady, taking out a lavender coloured hanky with a lace edge, and dabbing her eyes.

'Or to find out which way the wind is blowing,' said Jack the Sailor, and he took out a large blue handkerchief and held it up in the air. 'Sou'-westerly, today,' he said.

'Or to make a toy rabbit,' said Michael's sister Ann, and she folded her little pink handkerchief round her fingers into the shape of a rabbit.

'Or to make a flag to fly if the Queen or anyone important comes,' said Michael's friend, Billy, taking out an orange handkerchief and knotting two corners to a stick.

Little Hippo smiled. 'So a handkerchief really *would* be very useful even if I *didn't* catch a cold?' he said.

'Yes,' everyone agreed. Then Ann said, 'Here, you can have mine,' and she gave Little Hippo the pink rabbit handkerchief.

'And mine,' said Michael, handing him the green hanky.

'And mine,' said Tom the Postman, taking the knotted hanky off his head.

One by one they all gave Little Hippo their handkerchiefs.

'Ooh, *thank* you,' said Little Hippo, and he was so pleased he turned head over heels on the

31

grass. Then he ran home to show them all to his mother.

'Mother!' he called, 'Look at – at – at – ATISHOO!'

And Little Hippo sneezed loudly.

'Dear me,' his mother said. 'You've caught a cold! How lucky that I've just been to buy you a handkerchief,' and she gave Little Hippo a huge brown hanky and he sneezed into it three times: ATCHOO! ATCHOO! ATCHOO!

'I'll keep this one for colds,' said Little Hippo snuffily, 'and the others for other things. You know, mother, handkerchiefs can be *such* useful things . . . a – a – ATISHOOO!'

The guineapig show

Armorel Kay Walling

Are you sitting comfortably? Then I'll begin.

Daddy said, 'There's a Guineapig Show on the Common.'

'A show?' cried Rachel. 'Singing and dancing? Oh *please* can we go?'

'Guineapigs singing and dancing?' laughed Daddy. 'No, not *that* kind of show! It's a competition – to find the most beautiful guineapig and give it a prize.'

'What prize?'

'A big blue ribbon, I expect,' said Daddy.

Rachel thought. 'I have the most beautiful guineapig in the world,' she said. 'Can we put *her* in the show?'

'Why not?' said Daddy.

So Rachel fetched Sunset, her guineapig. Sunset didn't *look* like the most beautiful guineapig in the world just then. She'd been playing in the muddy grass.

'We must do her hair,' said Daddy.

He shook some special guineapig shampoo into a bowl of warm water. Sunset didn't like having her hair washed. She went 'weeeeeeeek!' She looked sort of *flat*, too. Rachel felt sorry for her. She gave her a carrot to cheer her up, and let her dry by the warm stove. Then she fetched her dolly's brush. She brushed Sunset until she shone. Sunset liked that. She closed her eyes and s-t-r-e-t-c-h-e-d. And then, when Daddy had filed all her toenails, she *did* look beautiful.

'But don't cry if she *doesn't* win the prize,' said Daddy.

There was a big tent on the Common. Inside the tent were lots of tables. And on the tables were lots of cages. And in the cages were lots of guineapigs: lots and lots – more than Rachel thought lived in the whole world; big ones, little ones, smooth ones, fluffy ones, black ones, white ones, some all different colours like Sunset, and some with so much fur you couldn't tell which end was which!

There were lots of people, too.

A lady asked Rachel how old Sunset was, and wrote her name in a book. She stuck a number on Sunset's ear, and put her in a cage. Then a man in a white coat came to look. He looked at every guineapig – at their fur, and ears, and toenails, and teeth.

He put them back in their cages, and thought.

Then he picked up a big blue ribbon. He walked over to where Rachel and her Daddy were standing. He went up to Sunset's cage and then . . . he pinned the ribbon *on the cage next door*.

'Don't cry, Daddy,' said Rachel quickly. 'I'll find another blue ribbon to put on Sunset's cage tomorrow. After all, *we* know she's still the most beautiful guineapig in the world, don't we?'

'We do!' said Daddy, and felt happy again. He let Rachel go on the swings on the way home, so *she* felt happy too.

But Sunset felt *very* happy. Because for tea Rachel gave her some oats, *and* apple *and* carrot *and* a dandelion – which, if you're a guineapig, is even better than winning the prize in a Guineapig Show!

Susie's hair ribbon

Malcolm Carrick

Are you sitting comfortably? Then I'll begin.

One day Susie decided to put her new pink hair ribbon in her hair. She looked around her room, but she couldn't see it anywhere.

'Oh bother,' Susie said, 'I'm always losing things!'

So she looked under her bed. She didn't find her hair ribbon, but she found the lid of her jewel box.

'I've been looking for that,' said Susie, and she put the lid back on her jewel box.

Then she looked through all her drawers for her hair ribbon. She didn't find the pink ribbon, but she did find five pence her aunt gave her last Christmas.

'I've been looking for that,' Susie said, and put it in her money box.

Then she looked under the carpet. She didn't find her hair ribbon, but she did find the key to her wind-up train.

'Oh, I've been looking for that,' she said as she put it with the train.

Next she turned out the wastepaper basket. Susie didn't find her hair ribbon, but she did find her doll's lost shoe.

'I've been looking for that,' she said, and put it on her doll's foot.

Susie thought her new pink hair ribbon might be in her school bag, so she turned that out. She didn't find the ribbon, but she did find the pencil sharpener she thought she had lost.

'I've been looking for that,' she said and went to put it in her school bag, but as it was there already, she went on searching for her hair ribbon.

'Perhaps it's in my doll's pram,' she thought, so she had a good rummage about in there. She didn't find the hair ribbon, but she did find the shiny medal her uncle had given her.

'I've been looking for that,' she said, and she put it in her doll's pram so that she would know where to find it again.

The last place she could think to look was in her toy box. She turned that out on the floor, but still she didn't find her hair ribbon. But she did find a frilly piece of lace that she'd been saving.

'I've been looking for that,' she said and put it in her sewing bag. Then she rushed downstairs.

'Mum,' she yelled, 'I've found the lid of my jewel box, and the key of my train, and five pence that Aunty gave me for Christmas, and my doll's shoe and my pencil sharpener, and Uncle's shiny medal, and my frilly piece of lace. But I still didn't find my new pink hair ribbon that I was looking for.'

'Well no wonder,' her Mum laughed. 'It's in your hair, Susie.'

Susie felt her hair, and there was the pink ribbon; it had been there all the time.

'I was looking for that,' she said.

Constantinople or the elephant who didn't like baths

Peter Ashley and Janey Gordon

Are you sitting comfortably? Then I'll begin.

Tom was playing in the living room, when an elephant's trunk came through the window.

'An elephant's trunk!' exclaimed Tom and, looking out of the window, he saw a small elephant.

'An elephant,' gasped Tom.

'What else do you expect to find at the end of a trunk?' said the elephant. 'My name is Constantinople.'

'I'm Tom,' said Tom. 'What are you doing here?'

'I've run away from the zoo, and you've got to hide me. My keeper will try to find me.'

Tom thought for a moment and then said, 'I've got some dressing-up clothes. Perhaps we could disguise you.'

Tom helped Constantinople in through the window.

'Shhhh, Constantinople, I don't want my

aunty to hear you,' said Tom. He was afraid that Aunty Alice, who was looking after him that day, might not be pleased by an elephant bouncing on to the sofa.

'Why have you run away?' Tom asked.

'I've got a new keeper and he makes me take a bath every day. I hate baths.'

'I know just how you feel,' agreed Tom.

Just then Constantinople saw his new keeper out in the street, coming towards the house.

'Quick,' he said, 'where's the disguise?'

'Here,' said Tom. 'Put on this bonnet and dress.'

Two minutes later the doorbell rang. Tom heard Aunty Alice open the door and a man's voice say, 'I saw my elephant coming this way. Do you mind if I look inside?'

Aunty Alice and the keeper came into the living room. Aunty Alice said to Tom, 'Have you seen an elephant?'

'I've been playing with my friend, Susan,' said Tom.

His 'friend Susan' was dressed in a big blue bonnet and a green dress with a gold belt.

'Bless my soul,' said the keeper. 'What big ears that girl's got.'

'It's very rude to make personal remarks,' said Aunty Alice, and they went out to look round the garden.

'Do you think he suspected?' said Constantinople as he took off the big blue bonnet.

'He might have,' said Tom. 'We'd better change your disguise. Put on Mummy's fur coat and stand on my skateboard.'

Two minutes later Tom heard Aunty Alice and the keeper come back into the house.

'Do you mind if I look in there again?' the keeper asked.

Aunty Alice and the keeper came into the living room. Aunty Alice said to Tom, 'Have you seen that elephant yet?'

'I've been playing with my toy dog, Woofa,' said Tom.

His 'toy dog Woofa' was brown and furry and was on wheels.

'Bless my soul,' said the keeper. 'What a long nose that dog's got.'

'They don't make toys like that any more,' said Aunty Alice, and they went out to look in the garage.

'Do you think he suspected?' said Constantinople as he took off Tom's mummy's fur coat.

'He might have,' said Tom. We'd better change your disguise. Put on this table cloth and kneel down.'

Two minutes later Tom heard Aunty Alice and the keeper come back into the house.

'Do you mind if I look in there one last time?'

the keeper asked.

Aunty Alice and the keeper came into the living room. Aunty Alice said to Tom, 'Any sign of that elephant yet?'

'I've been playing tea parties on my table,' said Tom.

His 'table' was a large lump with a red and white table-cloth on it, and a blue tea set all arranged for tea.

'Bless my soul,' said the keeper. 'What thick legs that table's got.'

'They don't make tables like that any more,' said Aunty Alice.

They were just going out to look in the kitchen when a big voice came from outside the window.

'Constantinople, Constantinople, where are you?'

When he heard this, Constantinople shouted, 'Mummy, Mummy,' and he rushed out from under the table-cloth, scattering the tea set all over the floor.

'I miss you, Mummy,' he cried as he bounced on the sofa, jumped out of the window and ran to his mummy, a large, grey elephant.

'Why did you run away?' his mummy said.

'I didn't want a bath every day,' said Constantinople.

Aunty Alice said, 'When Tom didn't like his baths, his mummy gave him some boats to play with in the water.'

'What a good idea,' the keeper said.

So Constantinople borrowed some of Tom's boats to play with in his bath, and he became the cleanest elephant in the zoo!

Constantinople goes shopping

Peter Ashley and Janey Gordon

Are you sitting comfortably? Then I'll begin.

Tom had a special friend, Constantinople, who was a little elephant. One day Tom's Aunty Alice took Tom and Constantinople to do some shopping at the supermarket. On the supermarket door was a notice which said –

> No Smoking
> No Prams
> No Dogs

'Upon my trunk,' Constantinople said. "No dogs.'

'That's all right,' said Tom. 'You're an elephant.'

Inside there were a lot of busy people carrying baskets or pushing their trolleys up and down the rows. Some mothers had their children in the trolleys.

'Can I have a ride?' Constantinople asked. And he climbed up on a trolley.

'You're too heavy,' said Tom. But it was too late.

CRRRRUNNNNCHHHHHHHH.

Constantinople squashed the trolley flat.

'Oh dear,' Aunty Alice sighed.

The supermarket manager, Mr Bargain-Price, came to see what the fuss was about.

'By Merthyr Tydfil!' he said. 'What a mess.'

'I'm sorry,' Constantinople said. 'I'll straighten it out.'

'And I'll help,' said Tom.

So they pulled and untwisted the wire trolley.

'I think I'll take a basket instead,' said Aunty Alice.

Tom asked Aunty Alice what was on her shopping list.

'The first thing,' she said, 'is a tin of baked beans.'

Constantinople looked along the shelf at all the different coloured tins.

'Here you are,' he said, going up to a tall stack of baked bean tins. He put out his trunk and, instead of taking a tin from the top, he took one from the bottom of the stack.

'Look out,' said Tom.

CRRRRRRAAAAASHHHHHH.

The whole lot came tumbling down and bounced all over the floor.

'Oh dear,' Aunty Alice sighed.

The supermarket manager, Mr Bargain-Price, came to see what the fuss was about.

'By Merthyr Tydfil and Abergavenny!' he said. 'What a mess.'

'I'm sorry,' Constantinople said. 'I'll pick them up.'

'And I'll help,' said Tom.

So they picked up all the tins and put them into a pile.

'I think I'll get spaghetti rings instead,' Aunty Alice said.

Tom asked Aunty Alice what was next on her shopping list.

'The second thing,' she said, 'is a packet of cornflakes.'

Constantinople looked along the shelf at all the different shaped packets.

'Here you are,' he said, picking up a packet. On the front of the packet it said 'Free Elephant'.

'Don't worry, elephant,' said Constantinople, 'I'll set you free. It's cruel to keep elephants in small boxes like that.'

RRRRRRRIPPPPPPPPPP.

He began to rip the box to pieces.

'It's only a tiny toy elephant that they give away free, for nothing,' said Tom.

The cornflakes were scattered about in the air like snow.

'Oh dear,' Aunty Alice sighed.

The supermarket manager, Mr Bargain-Price, came to see what the fuss was about.

'By Merthyr Tydfil, Abergavenny and Penrhyndeudraeth!' he said. 'What a mess.'

'I'm sorry,' Constantinople said. 'I'll clear it up.'

'And I'll help,' said Tom.

So they swept up all the cornflakes and bits of cardboard packet.

'I think I'll get porridge instead,' Aunty Alice said.

Tom asked Aunty Alice what was next on her shopping list.

'The third thing,' she said, 'is a box of soap powder.'

Constantinople looked along the shelf at all the different sized boxes.

'Here you are,' he said, picking up a very large box.

'That's much too big for me,' said Aunty Alice.

'It's just right for Constantinople,' Tom said. 'It's a jumbo pack!'

Just then, Mr Bargain-Price put on some

soothing music for his customers, to help them do their shopping.

'Upon my trunk,' yelled Constantinople, and leapt up into the air. 'Whenever I hear music I have to dance,' he said, grabbing Aunty Alice for a bossa nova.

Tom explained to the other customers that Constantinople's grandfather had been a circus elephant. That's why he was dancing.

'What a good idea,' they said. And soon all the other customers were doing the bossa nova too.

'Oh dear,' Aunty Alice panted.

The supermarket manager, Mr Bargain-Price, came to see what the fuss was about.

'By Merthyr Tydfil, Abergavenny, Penrhyn-deudraeth and Llanfairpwllgwyngyllgogerych-wyrndrobwllllantysiliogogogoch!!!' he said. 'This is too much.'

He went and turned the music off. Then he said to Aunty Alice, 'That elephant will have to go. At once. This instant. *Now.*'

Aunty Alice, Tom and Constantinople left.

They went home and they had tea. They were very hungry after all the dancing.

The next time Aunty Alice and Tom went to the supermarket, the notice on the door said –

No Smoking, No Prams, No Dogs, And Definitely *No Elephants*

Clever old foxy

Eugenie Summerfield

Are you sitting comfortably? Then I'll begin.

High up in the hills, quite hidden by the trees, lived an old foxy fox in his den. It was a lovely place to live. That old foxy fox could look down and see the stream where the ducks came to swim. He hardly ever came down to try and eat them! He would wink his eye and say,

'I bother nobody and nobody bothers me,
Because that's the way I like to be.'

Old Foxy was very happy with his way of life until one day along came a tickly, tetchy flea with his new little flea wife.

'Why my dear,' said Mr Flea to Mrs Flea, 'here's the very place for you and me to set up home and bring up a fine family.'

Together Mr Flea and Mrs Flea hopped up on old Foxy's back and settled down happily in the fox's warm golden fur.

At first old Foxy hardly noticed the fleas were there at all. He could still wink his eye and say,

'I bother nobody and nobody bothers me,
Because that's the way I like to be.'
But after a while, there weren't just Mr Flea
and Mrs Flea. There were hundreds of little fleas
– all very naughty and very noisy. They hopped
and they ran. From morning to night, they
quarrelled and they fought. They played football
and hide-and-seek. They held flea-circuses and
flea-markets. They tickled and tormented that
old Foxy from the top of his head to the tip of his
tail.

Old Foxy tried to reason with them.

'Please go away,' he said. 'I bother nobody, so
please don't bother me. That's the way I'd like to
be.'

But those naughty fleas just laughed and said,

'Ha ha, hee hee! You won't get rid of us that
easily!'

So old Foxy said to himself, 'I will have to think
of some way of getting rid of these troublesome
fleas.'

First he tried shaking himself very hard to
make them all fall off, but they didn't. They all
laughed and shouted,

'Ha ha, hee hee! You won't get rid of us so
easily!'

Then he tried rolling in the sand to rub them
out of his fur, but that didn't work either. Again
they all laughed and shouted,

'Ha ha, hee hee! You won't get rid of us so easily!'

So old Foxy lay down among the long cool grasses. He stayed quite still until a bright idea came to him. Then he jumped up and ran around under the trees. In his mouth he gathered up all the soft green moss he could find.

The little fleas were much too busy being as naughty and as noisy as usual to notice what old Foxy was doing. Still carrying the soft green moss in his mouth, old Foxy went down through the trees until he came to the stream. The ducks swimming there were afraid old Foxy had come to eat them.

'Quack quack ducky dear, what shall we do?'

'Has old Foxy come to make a meal of me, or of you?'

But old Foxy didn't even look at the ducks. He turned his back upon them.

The ducks watched old Foxy walking backwards into the water carrying the moss in his mouth.

'Quack quack ducky dear, what is he up to?'

They decided it was safer for them not to stay. So the ducks flew away at once. Old Foxy waded deeper and deeper into the stream. The water nearly covered his back and all the naughty, noisy fleas on old Foxy's back shouted,

'Ha ha, hee hee! You won't get rid of us so easily!'

They hopped off old Foxy's back and up on to his nose.

But soon the water had reached old Foxy's nose. The fleas didn't like this one little bit. They ran round and round trying to keep out of the water. Until one of them saw the piece of moss in old Foxy's mouth.

'Look! If we all jump on to that soft green moss, we'll be as safe and snug as bugs in a rug. This old foxy fox can't get rid of us that easily!'

All together the fleas hopped on to the moss. Just as the very last one leapt off his nose, Old Foxy opened his mouth and let the moss, and all the fleas with it, float away down the stream.

He winked his eye and said,

'I bother nobody and nobody bothers me,
Because that's the way I like to be.'

Then he swam back to the water's edge. He climbed out and shook himself dry. Old Foxy went back to his den among the hills where he danced and sang all by himself in the sunlight.

The dog who had
no name

Leila Berg

Are you sitting comfortably? Then I'll begin.

Once upon a time there was a dog.

He was a very jolly dog, a yellow dog, and his nose was black. He had two white paws and two brown paws. But he had no name at all. One day this little yellow dog said to himself, 'Everybody has a name but me. I shall go off and find a name.' So off he went. Patter, patter, patter, patter on his neat little feet.

He pattered down the street, and he passed some men mending the road. 'Hello, little yellow dog,' shouted the road men. 'Where are you off to, in such a hurry?'

'I'm off to find my name,' said the little yellow dog.

'Stop a minute,' cried the road men. 'Is Pat your name?'

'No, Pat isn't my name,' said the little yellow dog. And on he went. Patter, patter, patter, patter on his neat little feet.

He pattered down the street, till he passed a lady buying bread. 'Hello little yellow dog,' said the lady. 'Where are you running so far away?'

'I'm off to find my name,' said the little yellow dog.

'Wait a bit,' cried the lady. 'Is Bess your name?'

'Oh no, Bess isn't my name,' said the little yellow dog. And on he went. Patter, patter, patter, patter on his neat little feet.

On he pattered till he came to a window-cleaner, carrying a ladder. 'Hello, little yellow dog,' cried the window-cleaner. 'Where are you off to, this fine day?'

'I'm off to find my name,' said the little yellow dog.

'Don't go so fast,' said the window-cleaner. 'Is Gyp your name?'

'No, Gyp isn't my name,' said the little yellow dog. And on he went. Patter, patter, patter, patter on his neat little feet.

On he pattered till he came to a postman carrying letters. 'Hello little yellow dog,' said the postman. 'Where are you going, at such a rate?'

'I'm going to find my name,' said the little yellow dog.

'Is Rough your name?' asked the postman.

'No, Rough isn't my name,' said the little yellow dog. And on he went. Patter, patter, patter, patter on his neat little feet. On he pattered till he was tired out. Then he sat down on the pavement at the side of the road, and he stuck out his tongue.

And he huffed, and he huffed, and he huffed.

'Oh!' he said – 'OH-oh-oh. I'll – never – never – never – never – find – my – name. Oh-oh-oh.'

Just then two little children came along. A boy and a girl. 'Hello, little yellow dog,' said the boy and girl. 'You look quite tired out. Whatever have you been doing?'

'Huff, huff, huff,' said the little yellow dog, 'I've been looking for my name – huff – but I haven't found it yet – huff – and I'm very tired – huff, huff, huff.'

'Wait a minute,' said the children. 'Don't go away. Is Trix your name? Is it Trix?'

The little dog thought for a moment. First he put his head on one side and thought that way. Then he put his head on the other side, and thought that way. Then he stood up and wagged his tail. Then he turned round quickly three times and barked, yap, yap.

'Yes,' he said. 'It *is*. Trix *is* my name. Yap, yap!'

'Hooray,' shouted the children. 'Then you can come with us. Come on, Trix.'

And off they ran, shouting and singing and barking. The little girl, the little boy and the little yellow dog.

Fingy and the garden

Diana Webb

Are you sitting comfortably? Then I'll begin.

Susie's favourite toy was a little woolly man who fitted neatly on her finger. His name was Fingy and he had yellow hair and a blue and red striped suit.

One afternoon Susie went for a walk in the country with Fingy in her pocket. She skipped along behind Mummy and Daddy as they rambled through a wood, down a hill with cottages on either side and into a leafy lane. When they turned the corner at the end of the lane they began to walk beside a long high wall built of red brick.

'What's on the other side of that wall, Daddy?' asked Susie.

'Someone's garden and house I expect,' said Daddy.

'It must be a very big garden. Does the Queen live there?' asked Susie.

'I don't think so,' said Daddy.

'If you lifted me up on your shoulder,' said Susie, 'I think I would be able to see into the garden.'

'Oh no,' said Daddy firmly. 'I can't do that. That would be nosey.'

Susie was very disappointed. Mummy and Daddy walked a little further and sat down for a rest on the grass by the side of the road while Susie dawdled along looking up at the wall.

Suddenly she saw a very long twig lying on the ground and she had a wonderful idea. She took Fingy out of her pocket and said, 'Fingy, I'm going to put you on the end of this twig and then I'm going to stand on tiptoe and hold the twig as high above my head as I can, so you will be able to see over the wall and tell me what is on the other side.'

'I don't want to be nosey,' said Fingy uncertainly.

'It's all right,' said Susie. 'That little bird sitting on the wall can see into the garden, but he isn't being nosey is he?'

'Isn't he?' said Fingy.

'No of course not,' said Susie. 'Come on Fingy.'

She fitted him on to the end of the twig and held it up in the air. Then she stood on tiptoe and stretched as high as she could.

'Can you see over the wall, Fingy?' she asked breathlessly.

'Just about,' said Fingy.

'What can you see?' asked Susie, feeling very excited.

'I can see a man mowing the lawn with a shiny silver lawnmower,' said Fingy.

'And what else?' gasped Susie.

'I can see a big tree with beautiful red flowers shaped like bells. There are four people sitting under the tree in wicker chairs, eating enormous gigantic strawberries.'

'Who are they?' cried Susie. 'Tell me who they are.'

'There is a pirate. He is feeding his parrot with one of the strawberries. Next to him there is a clown. He is sticking one of the strawberries on the end of his nose. And next to him there is a wizard. He is waving his hands over one of the strawberries. I think he is trying to change it into something.'

'Is there anyone else?' squeaked Susie.

'There is a lady, she is eating her strawberries sensibly,' said Fingy.

'Who is the lady? Is it the Queen?' Susie was so excited that she jumped up and down. 'Is it the Queen, Fingy? Is it the Queen?'

Before Fingy could answer, Susie jumped up and down so much that she tossed poor Fingy right off the top of the twig, over the wall and into the garden.

She stared for a long time at the bare end of the twig where Fingy had been sitting. Then she started to cry. She cried and she cried until suddenly she saw something shoot up above the top of the wall. When she rubbed her tears away she saw that somebody on the other side of the wall had lifted a twig high in the air, and Fingy was perched on top of it. Susie quickly picked up her own twig, raised it up to the wall and carefully hoisted Fingy off the end of the other person's twig. Soon she was clutching Fingy tightly in her hand again.

She stared at the wall and opened her mouth to say to the person on the other side, 'Are you the Queen?' but she was too shy, so she just whispered, 'Thank you very much,' and ran to find her Mummy and Daddy.

When she stopped running she said to Fingy, 'Was it the Queen in that garden?' Fingy moved his head, but Susie wasn't quite sure whether he meant 'Yes' or 'No'.

Fingy and the magic stone

Diana Webb

Are you sitting comfortably? Then I'll begin.

One afternoon when the sun was shining, Susie went to some woods for a picnic. In the woods there was a stone that was as big as a car. It was covered in moss and it looked like a huge grey and green frog.

'Do you think that's a magic stone?' Susie asked her Daddy.

'I don't know,' said Daddy, 'I suppose it might be.'

'But do you think it is?' said Susie.

'I really don't know,' said Daddy.

Susie walked up to the stone. She walked

round it but she was careful not to touch it. Then she hid behind the stone and took Fingy out of her pocket.

'If you touch that stone you're silly,' she told him.

'Why?' said Fingy.

'Because it's a magic stone,' said Susie.

'I don't mind touching it,' said Fingy.

'But it might put a spell on you,' said Susie.

'It might put a *good* spell on me,' said Fingy.

Susie looked at the stone and she looked at Fingy. 'Are you sure you don't mind touching it?' she said.

'I don't mind at all,' said Fingy.

Susie started to pull Fingy off her finger, but she didn't pull him right off. She pulled him until only his feet were touching the end of her finger. Then she reached out slowly, and very quickly she touched the stone with the top of Fingy's head. For a moment she was frightened that he might disappear, but he just smiled back at Susie.

'It didn't hurt,' said Fingy. 'I feel all special and magic now.'

Susie ran to her Daddy.

'Fingy touched the magic stone,' she shouted.

'Did he really?' said Daddy.

'Yes he did,' said Susie, 'so do you think he's lucky now?'

'I have no idea,' said Daddy.

'How can I find out?' asked Susie.

'I don't know,' said Daddy.

Susie stared at Fingy and Fingy stared at Susie and they both thought very hard.

'Point me straight ahead of you,' said Fingy, 'and I'll lead you to some treasure.'

So Susie pointed Fingy in front of her and they went for a walk among the trees. They walked round and round in circles.

'Why are we walking round and round in circles?' said Susie.

'We're looking for treasure,' said Fingy.

'I don't think that stone made you lucky at all,' said Susie. 'I don't think that you're going to find anything.'

'Yes I am,' said Fingy. 'You must shut your eyes now, and turn round three times with your arms stretched out, and when you stop you must look where I'm pointing and walk three steps in that direction.'

Susie did as she was told, but she couldn't see any treasure when she stopped.

'Now you must do it again,' said Fingy.

So Susie did it again, but she still couldn't see any treasure.

'*And* you must do it again,' said Fingy.

So Susie did it once more.

'I'm pointing straight to the treasure now,' said Fingy, 'but you might have to walk a long way to find it.'

Susie sighed. Very slowly she followed Fingy in a straight line. She had to walk slowly because she was staring at the ground.

'What are you doing?' said Daddy.

'Ssh,' said Susie. 'I'm looking for treasure.' She bent nearer and nearer to the ground until she was pushing Fingy along on the path. The top of his head became rather dirty.

'Look,' said Fingy suddenly. 'I've found it.'

There on the ground in front of him was a shiny silver fifty-pence piece.

Susie was very excited. She gazed at the fifty-pence piece. Then she picked it up.

'The stone did make you lucky Fingy,' she said. 'It must have been magic.'

'Fingys are *always* lucky,' said Fingy.

A hat for Bethan

Gill Davies

Are you sitting comfortably? Then I'll begin.

Bethan wanted a hat. She watched the postman with his smart, peaked cap as he pushed letters through the letter-boxes all along the road.

'Can I have a hat, please?' she said.

Mummy was washing up. She popped a plastic cup upside down on Bethan's head.

'There,' she said, 'a hat!'

But Bethan knew that wouldn't do. So she shook her head – and the plastic cup fell, clatter bang, on to the kitchen floor.

'I would like a hat,' said Bethan, as they sat on the bus, going to visit Gran. The bus driver had a lovely blue squashy hat with a red edge – and a money bag, too. Mummy smiled. She tied her scarf round Bethan's head.

'There,' she said, 'a hat!'

But the knot hurt Bethan's neck and she knew that wouldn't do.

'Please give me a hat,' said Bethan, as they sat

drinking tea at Gran's. Grandpa folded his newspaper into a triangle and popped it on Bethan's head.

'There,' he said, 'a hat!'

But when Bethan stood up the hat slipped right down over her nose and she trod on the cat. That wouldn't do, either.

'Please can I try on your hat?' Bethan asked a policeman in town, but the policeman said sadly he wasn't allowed to take it off, that it was far too heavy anyway, and that it made even his strong head ache by the end of the day.

'Please can I try on your hat?' Bethan asked the chef in the café.

'It's far too full of flour,' he wheezed. He shook his head, and great clouds of white dust flew into the air and made Bethan sneeze.

'Please can I try on your hat?' Bethan asked the fireman.

'Oh no, my lovely,' said the fireman, 'I keep my sandwiches inside it!' And he raised his helmet to show Bethan his lunch.

'I want a hat,' said Bethan.

'I know,' said Mummy.

'Say "please",' said Daddy.

'Please,' said Bethan.

'Well, here you are then!' said Mummy.

And there, in Mummy's hand, was a beautiful blue and red striped hat, with a white fluffy pom-

pom on the top. At last! A hat for Bethan.

'I've got a hat,' said Bethan.

'I've got a hat,' said Bethan, to everyone she saw.

'I know,' said the postman.

'I know,' said the bus conductor.

'I know,' said Gran, and Grandpa, and the policeman, and the chef, and the fireman, 'I know, and a fine hat it is too, Bethan. Aren't you lucky?'

'Fraidy mouse

Anne Wellington

Are you sitting comfortably? Then I'll begin.

Once upon a time there were three grey mice. And they lived in a corner of a barn.

Two of the mice weren't afraid of anything, except the brown tabby cat who lived in the farmhouse. Two of the mice said, 'Hi! Look at us. We're tricky and we're quicky and we're fighty and we're bitey. We're not afraid of anything, except the tabby cat.'

But the third little mouse said, 'Don't look at me. I'm quivery and quaky and shivery and shaky. I'm afraid of everything. I'm a 'Fraidy Mouse.'

'Fraidy Mouse's brothers said, 'Don't be

ridiculous. There's nothing to be frightened of, except the tabby cat.'

'Fraidy Mouse shivered, 'I've never seen a tabby cat. Does Tabby Cat stamp with his feet? Does he growl?'

'Fraidy Mouse's brothers said, 'Don't be absurd. Tabby Cat sits by the door of the barn.

> He sits on the ground,
> He's big and he's round.
> He doesn't move a muscle
> Till he hears a little rustle.
> Then he'll jump. Thump!
> And he'll eat you till you're dead.'

Then 'Fraidy Mouse's brothers said, 'But Tabby Cat's indoors now. So off we go together to be bold, brave mice.'

'Fraidy Mouse was left alone, sitting in the barn. In case he should see something fearsome and frightening, he closed his eyes tightly and fell fast asleep.

While 'Fraidy Mouse was sleeping, the farmer passed the barn. He was carrying a sack full of big brown potatoes. One of the potatoes fell out and rolled about. It rolled to the door of the barn. And there it stayed.

'Fraidy Mouse woke up. He saw that big potato! 'Mercy me! It's Tabby Cat, sitting by the door!

He's sitting on the ground,
And he's big and he's round.
He won't move a muscle
Till he hears a little rustle.
Then he'll jump. Thump!
And he'll eat me till I'm dead.'

'Fraidy Mouse kept so still that all his bones were aching. Then his brothers came back, and they said, 'Hi, 'Fraidy Mouse!'

'Fraidy Mouse whispered, 'Hush! Oh hush! Don't you see the tabby cat sitting by the door?'

'Fraidy Mouse's brothers said, 'Don't be idiotic. That's not a tabby cat. That's a big potato.' And they laughed. 'Fraidy Mouse's brothers rolled around laughing, until they were exhausted and had to go to sleep.

But poor little 'Fraidy Mouse cried himself to sleep.

While the mice were sleeping, the farmer passed the barn. He picked the potato up and carried it away. 'Fraidy Mouse twitched in his sleep – dreaming. He dreamed he was a tricky, quicky little mouse.

As the sun went down, the big brown tabby cat came padding to the barn. And he sat by the door. 'Fraidy Mouse twitched in his sleep again – dreaming. He dreamed he was a fighty, bitey little mouse.

After a while, the mice woke up. The first thing

they saw in the twilight was the cat, a big round brown thing sitting by the door. 'Fraidy Mouse's brothers hid away in holes. They stared out with frightened eyes, too terrified to speak.

'Fraidy Mouse thought they were teasing him again, pretending to be frightened of a big brown potato. He wouldn't get caught like *that* again!

He called out, 'Hi there! You silly old potato!' The tabby cat was so surprised he didn't move a muscle. 'Fraidy Mouse called again, 'I'm only small and 'Fraidy. But I'm not afraid of *you*, you silly old potato. And neither are my tricky, quicky, fighty, bitey brothers.'

Tabby Cat said to himself, 'What a mouse! If that's a little 'Fraidy Mouse, the smallest, most afraid mouse, his brothers must be terrible. I shan't come here again'.

Then Tabby Cat stalked away, pretending not to hurry. And 'Fraidy Mouse said, 'Funny! That potato's got a tail!'

'Fraidy Mouse's tricky, quicky, fighty, bitey brothers came creeping from their holes, and they said, 'Oh 'Fraidy Mouse! How brave you were to talk to the tabby cat like that!'

'Fraidy Mouse thought, 'Tabby Cat! That wasn't a potato. I was talking to a real live tabby cat. Oh my!'

Then his legs gave way, and he fell on his back. And his brothers said, 'He's resting. It's tiring being so brave!'

The ballad of Bad Belinda

Moira Miller

Are you sitting comfortably? Then I'll begin.

I'll tell you a story, I promise it's true,
Of a Horrible Child – it couldn't be you!
Her name was Belinda Samantha de Vere,
And her Terrible Tale is quite shocking to hear.

Now Belinda was known the length of the street
As the sort of child you would *hate* to meet,
And mothers would say as they saw her pass by,
'There's Dreadful Belinda! I simply must fly
To take in the cat, or she'll start having fits.
Belinda has frightened her out of her wits!'
For that Terrible Child was a *most awful tease,*
And actually thought it 'a jolly good wheeze'
To tie an old tin to the long furry tail
Of a cat who lay sleeping on top of the wall.
She would then yell 'Ya-Boo!' at the top of her
  voice,
And up leapt the cat – what a horrible noise!

Clanking and banging and yowling and screaming.
She thought it was funny, and found it quite
  pleasing
That people were so upset by her teasing.
She pestered the Baby, asleep in his pram;
Stuffed a hairbrush in bed with her Big Brother
  Sam,
Who woke with a start and jumped out with a
  yell,
'There's a hedgehog in bed! I know I can tell.
I felt all its bristles. I'm sure that it wiggled!'
Dreadful Belinda just giggled and giggled.

Her mother would scold and her father would
  shout,
But that Horrible Child was never put out.
She went on and on being Dreadfully Naughty,
Until the arrival of – Great Aunt Dotty.

This lady arrived on the doorstep one day,
And announced to the Family, 'I'm coming to
  stay.
The doctor has told me to have a good rest,
And a peaceful holiday here would be best.'
Now Belinda's Mum didn't have a Great Aunt,
And her Father, when questioned, admitted, 'I
  can't
Recall any mention of such a relation.
However she's here, and her bag's at the station.'

So they sent for her luggage and round came a
  porter,
A stout chap with whiskers, who said, 'I ain't
  never
Seen a lady wiv so much stuff!
There's 'at boxes, suit-cases, trunks and a muff
Of 'orrible fur – striped black, white and tan.'
'That's my cat,' said Aunt Dotty, 'you Foolish
  Young Man!'
'A cat!' thought Belinda: that Terrible Infant
Was planning all sorts of tricks in an instant.
She smiled at the cat with a horrible leer,
But the animal simply replied with a sneer.
He stretched and yawned a most elegant yawn,
And curled up to sleep on the front garden lawn.

Aunt Dotty by now was enjoying a cuppa
And ordering sardines on toast for her supper.
It was whilst she was nibbling at this tasty snack
That Belinda crept up to the room at the back,
The second-best bedroom – reserved for a guest.
(Belinda's Mother and Dad had the best!)
Here were Aunt Dotty's bags, all neatly stacked,
None of them being, as yet, unpacked.
Belinda – Bad Child – can you guess what she
  did?
Saw that hat-box on top, so she lifted the lid,
Intending, I'm sure there's no doubt of that,
To hide her pet mouse in Aunt Dotty's best hat.

But she dropped the lid with a terrible shout
As a huge hairy Jack-In-The-Box shot out!
Mother and Dad heard the rumpus of course,
And rushed up the stairs to discover the source.
Aunt Dotty just smiled and hitched up her cloak,
And muttered, 'What? Can't the child take a
    joke?'

Next morning at breakfast Belinda sat down
To a large boiled egg, a most beautiful brown.
Freckled and speckled, it looked really good.
A tasty boiled egg was her favourite food.
She picked up her spoon and tapped on the shell –
It was empty inside! Aunt Dotty said, 'Well!
Now there's a surprise you didn't foresee.
Just one of my little jokes. Now have some tea.'
But the cup that she handed that Terrible Child
Was salted, not sugared, and oh how she wailed!
Her Big Brother Sam, getting on with his meal,
Said, 'Serves you quite right. Now you know how
    we feel
When we have to put up with the tricks that *you*
    play.'
At this Our Belinda had nothing to say.

She stamped out to the shed feeling wickedly
    Naughty,
To plan her revenge on Great Aunt Dotty.
She was sitting there thinking some Terrible
    Thinks

When a dirty great spider came down through
the chinks
In the roof of that rickety old garden shed.
It landed – precisely – on top of her head.
Belinda sat, terrified, fixed to her stool,
Till she noticed a label that read APRIL FOOL!
There was also another with MADE IN HONG
KONG.
That spider was plastic! Could he belong
To Aunt Dotty's collection of Horrible Tricks?
'You bet,' groaned Belinda, and wondered,
'What next?'

The week dragged on getting worse and worse.
Great Aunt Dot was a Terrible Curse.
Belinda discovered her shoes full of jam,
And a wheel unscrewed from the Baby's pram
When Belinda was taking him out for his walk.
She'd to carry him home, which wasn't a joke!
The Baby, you see, didn't like being carried,
And wanted to crawl, so he struggled and
worried
And pulled at her pigtails till, all in a muddle,
Belinda and Baby both fell in a puddle.
They struggled back home, very tired and dirty,
And Belinda's Mum was really quite shirty.

At last, at the end of this Terrible Week,
Belinda was feeling thoroughly sick.
'If only she'd *go*,' wailed the Poor Child in pain,

'I'd never tease anyone EVER AGAIN!'
(Aunt Dotty had planted a drawing-pin
On the seat of her chair before she came in.)
'Did I hear aright?' said Great Aunt Dot.
'You'll never tease anyone – even the cat?'
'Oh Truly, Aunt Dot!' sobbed Belinda, and so
Aunt Dot went upstairs and got ready to go.

'But always remember,' she said as she packed,
'Any more nonsense and – *I'll be right back*!'

The giant brothers and the army

Val Annan

Are you sitting comfortably? Then I'll begin.

Giant Huster and Giant Bluster were twin brothers who were very wicked – they were always up to naughty tricks. One day, when they had been very, very bad, they were caught by the scruff of their necks and thrown out of Giantland!

'Be off with you, you terrible twins – and don't bother to come back until you are nice giants!' the other giants said.

'Bah!' yelled Huster and Bluster angrily, as they stamped away.

At first, the twin giants had a wonderful time – tearing up trees, blocking up streams and rivers and causing no end of wicked damage everywhere they went. Then, one day at around four o'clock when all good giants were at home having their tea, Huster and Bluster stood on top of a cold mountain. Far below them, they saw a little town where little people were hurrying this way and that.

Huster yelled at them, 'Hey! You down there . . . . Look at us! We are Giants Huster and Bluster!'

'And we want out tea!' said Bluster. 'Send it up to us or it will be the worse for you! We want two hundred boiled eggs, four hundred slices of buttered toast and ninety-three buckets of tea!'

The people in the little town quickly gathered around their Lord Mayor.

'What can we do?' they wailed. 'Our town isn't big enough to have such giant visitors – they will eat us out of house and home.'

The Lord Mayor looked thoughtful. 'We must give them their tea, or they might eat us! Perhaps they'll go away if we give them what they want!'

So, Huster and Bluster sat on top of the mountain and they had two hundred boiled eggs, four hundred slices of buttered toast and ninety-three buckets of tea.

'Hmm . . . that's better,' said Huster smacking his lips and rubbing his tummy.

'But we'll want the same again for breakfast

tomorrow – and a roast turkey lunch!' said Bluster.

'I'm afraid that isn't possible,' replied the little Mayor. 'Our food is needed for our um . . . Army!'

'Army!' roared Huster. 'I see no soldiers!'

'No, I see no soldiers and that means there is no Army!' said Bluster.

'Our soldiers are away at the moment – giant hunting – but they'll be back tomorrow – so you'd better be off while you can,' said the little Mayor.

'Bah!' said Huster.

'Bah!' said Bluster. 'We don't believe you. We shall wait to see this army of yours. But now, we'll have a good night's sleep in this big cave on your mountain. Be off with you! Army indeed!'

So the little people went back to the town and looked sadly at the Mayor.

'Where can we get an Army from at such short notice?' they wailed.

The Lord Mayor sighed, and looked up at the wintry sky. A big white snowflake drifted down and touched him lightly on the nose.

'Why! It's snowing!' he laughed. 'Quickly, everyone get out your shovels and spades – we must all make ten snowmen!'

And the little people worked all through the night – building snowmen!

Then they got out their pots of paint and they painted uniforms on the snowmen! The people gave them sticks and broom handles for guns.

Next morning when Huster and Bluster woke up they could hardly believe their eyes. All over the town and at the foot of the mountain were soldiers in red and white uniforms! They were all holding guns and did not look at all friendly.

Of course the twin giants didn't realize the soldiers were only made of snow.

'The Army is here!' gasped Huster. 'There are hundreds and hundreds of soldiers down there!'

Very frightened, Bluster said, 'I'm going back to Giantland this minute!'

'So am I!' said Huster.

And the giants twins ran all the way home.

They banged hard on the gates to Giantland, squealing, 'Please let us in – the Army is after us . . . please let us in!'

'Only if you promise to be good giants from now on,' said a booming voice from behind the gate.

'We promise! We promise!' squealed Huster and Bluster.

And they were good from that day on!

Young hedgehog helps rabbit

Vera Rushbrooke

Are you sitting comfortably? Then I'll begin.

Young Hedgehog and Rabbit were sitting by the hedge in the freshness of the early morning. Drops of dew were sparkling in the cobwebs stretched along the hedge, the birds were singing and everything was lovely.

Rabbit was saying, 'I feel so tired today! I don't know why. I don't work hard like Mole, digging out all those tunnels of his. And I don't run for miles like Red Fox when the dogs are after him. I don't even trot round the field like you do.'

'In fact,' chuckled Young Hedgehog, 'you're a lazy sort of fellow! Still, it's nice lazing about sometimes and listening to the bees humming, and smelling the honeysuckle in the hedge and the meadowsweet in the ditch, and just looking at things. Perhaps you feel tired because it's that sort of a morning, or maybe you didn't sleep well.'

'The trouble is,' said Rabbit, 'I heard there are

some nice juicy dandelions at the end of the next field, and I did fancy some. There aren't any around here. But I'm just too tired to go all that way.'

'You know,' said Young Hedgehog, 'once I felt like going for a trot to the wood, but it's rather a long way and I was tired, so I closed my eyes and *imagined* I went to the wood.

I kept talking to myself like this – Now I'm trotting over the daisy field till I come to the gate. Now I'm squeezing through the hedge where Mother Blackbird has her nest – and so on, till I *imagined* I'd got to the wood. It seemed so *real*, and all the time there I was sitting by the hedge with my eyes closed! Why don't you try it?'

'You really felt you'd been there?' asked Rabbit, 'just by closing your eyes and *thinking* it?'

'Yes,' said Young Hedgehog. 'You try it. Go on, sit down and close your eyes.'

'All right,' said Rabbit, and he sat down and closed his eyes.

'Now,' said Young Hedgehog, 'you want to go to the end of the next field, that's right?'

'Yes,' said Rabbit.

'Right,' said Young Hedgehog. 'Now, you know the way, so off we go, hoppity hop, over the daisy field.'

'Over the daisy field,' said Rabbit, with his eyes shut tight.

'And now,' Young Hedgehog said, 'you've got to the hedge. Can you squeeze through into the next field?'

'Yes,' said Rabbit, screwing up his nose as though he was trying hard.

'Are you through?' asked Young Hedgehog.

'Yes,' said Rabbit.

'Bit of a tough job, that, wasn't it?' Young Hedgehog said. 'Never mind, you're through now and in the next field. It's going to be difficult because the farmer's tractor has been over it, but off we go, hoppity hop!'

'Hoppity hop,' said Rabbit, his eyes tightly shut and not moving an inch.

'How rough the soil is now the tractor has turned it over,' said Young Hedgehog. 'Would you rather go round by the hedge?'

'It would be easier,' said Rabbit.

'Right!' said Young Hedgehog. 'Off we go.'

'Off we go!' Rabbit said, screwing up his eyes and imagining.

'Nearly there now,' said Young Hedgehog, 'mind you don't fall over the branches the wind has blown from the sycamore tree.'

'Right!' said Rabbit.

'Here we are,' said Young Hedgehog, 'at the end of the next field, where you wanted to go.'

'Can I open my eyes now?' asked Rabbit.

'No!' cried Young Hedgehog. 'You've got to go

back home. Come on, round by the hedge again. Mind the branches! Big ones, aren't they?'

'Yes,' Rabbit said, still with his eyes closed tight.

'Now, squeeze back through the hedge into the daisy field again,' said Young Hedgehog. 'Are you through?'

'Yes,' said Rabbit.

'Good!' Young Hedgehog said. 'Now over the daisy field and back home.'

'Can I open my eyes now?' asked Rabbit.

'Oh yes,' said Young Hedgehog.

Rabbit opened his eyes and blinked in the light.

'That was easy, wasn't it?' chuckled Young Hedgehog.

'Yes,' laughed Rabbit. 'All that way, and I didn't move an inch!' But suddenly he stopped laughing and began to look angry.

'What's the matter?' asked Young Hedgehog.

'What's the matter?' stormed Rabbit. 'I'll tell you what's the matter! We forgot the dandelions! That's all I wanted to go for!' And Rabbit hopped off to look for something to eat, muttering to himself, 'That Young Hedgehog and his stupid ideas!'

While Young Hedgehog just chuckled and said, 'I only tried to help!'

Teddy bear gets too fat
for his jacket

Margaret Gore

Are you sitting comfortably? Then I'll begin.

One morning when Teddy Bear was doing up his dark blue jacket with the three brass buttons, one of the buttons popped off and fell on the floor. It was the middle button.

'Oh dear,' said Teddy Bear in his deep, growly voice. 'I must be getting fat.'

He looked at himself in the mirror.

'Either I have got fat or the jacket has shrunk. Perhaps it shrank when I got caught in all that rain the other day.' Then Teddy Bear remembered he had been wearing his green pullover that day. So it wasn't that.

'There is no doubt about it,' said Teddy Bear. 'I have got too fat, and I shall have to do some exercises.'

But by the time Teddy Bear had done arms stretch three times, and knees bend twice, he was quite out of breath. 'Oh dear,' he growled. '*That* won't do. I shall have to think of something else. Perhaps my friend Badger, who lives on the common, can help me.'

So down to the common went Teddy Bear – left, right, left, right, left, right. He found Badger busily digging in the earth.

'Please, Badger, can you help me?' asked Teddy Bear. 'I have got too fat and I can't do up my jacket.'

'You should try digging holes as I do, Teddy Bear,' said Badger, and went on with his digging.

So Teddy Bear took off his jacket with the two buttons on instead of three, and began digging. He was tired out after digging up only about one pailful of earth.

'Oh dear,' growled Teddy Bear. '*That* won't do. I don't think bears are meant to dig holes. I'll have to think of something else. Perhaps my friend Brown Dog, who lives at the crossroads, can help me.'

So off went Teddy Bear again, left, right, left, right, till he came to the crossroads. Brown Dog lived in the house on the corner, and there he was, running about in his big garden.

'Please can you help me, Brown Dog?' asked Teddy Bear. 'I have got too fat and I can't do up my jacket.'

'You should do as I do, Teddy Bear,' replied Brown Dog. 'I am always running about – I hardly ever stop, except when I go to bed.'

So Teddy Bear ran all the way home without stopping once for a rest, but when he arrived he was so breathless he had to sit down in his armchair and have a few spoonfuls from a tin of sweet milk to make him feel better.

'Oh dear,' growled Teddy Bear. '*That* won't do. I don't think bears are meant to keep on running all the time without stopping. I'll have to think of something else. Perhaps my friend Tabcat will be able to help me.'

Down the road he went again, left, right, left, right, till he came to Tabcat's house. He saw Tabcat sitting on top of the high wall that went round his garden.

'Can you help me, Tabcat?' asked Teddy Bear. 'I have got too fat and I can't do up my jacket.'

'You should try jumping, Teddy Bear,' replied Tabcat, looking down at him with his green eyes. 'I am always jumping up on to this wall.'

'Jumping?' said Teddy Bear, doubtfully.

Tabcat looked at Teddy Bear's fat little figure standing there, and he said kindly, 'Perhaps you should start jumping on to *little* walls first, Teddy Bear. Come with me – I'll show you where there's one.'

Tabcat jumped gracefully down from the high wall and led Teddy Bear into the rose-garden.

'There you are, Teddy Bear, there's a nice *low* wall,' said Tabcat. 'Now if you'll excuse me, it's time for my lunch.'

It may have been a low wall to Tabcat, but to Teddy Bear it looked quite high. However, he went back a few steps, then took a flying leap at the wall. Unfortunately he didn't jump quite high enough, and he landed on the ground with a hard thud.

'Ooooo! Oh dear,' growled Teddy Bear. 'I *certainly* don't think bears were meant to go jumping up on to walls – even if they are only low ones.'

He walked sadly back home, feeling rather stiff and sore. On the way he came to Mrs Duck's shop. Once a week he always bought a large jar of honey at Mrs Duck's shop, and today was the day for it.

'It's no use,' he said to himself. 'The only way I shall stop being fat is to give up eating sweet things. I must go in and tell Mrs Duck that I shall not be needing any more jars of honey. Oh dear!'

He gave a big sigh, for if there was one thing Teddy Bear did love it was honey. But he bravely pushed open the shop door and went in.

'My goodness, Teddy Bear, you do look tired,' exclaimed Mrs Duck, and she made him sit down on a chair.

'I do feel rather weak, Mrs Duck,' replied Teddy Bear, and he cast a longing glance at a jar of honey on the shelf.

'Poor Teddy Bear, you probably need something to eat. I'll give you a big cup of cocoa and a chocolate biscuit. Then you'll feel better.'

Teddy Bear held up a weak paw.

'No, no thank you, Mrs Duck, I won't have anything,' he said. 'Not *anything*.'

Mrs Duck stared at Teddy Bear in astonishment.

'You must be ill, Teddy Bear,' she said. 'Perhaps I should call the doctor?'

Then Teddy Bear told her all his troubles, and showed her his jacket. 'The middle button came right off this morning,' he said, 'because I am getting too fat.'

'Nonsense, Teddy Bear,' laughed Mrs Duck. 'It only means you are growing up into a fine big bear – and who ever heard of a *thin* bear?

'Now you just stay there, and while you're drinking that cup of cocoa and eating that chocolate biscuit I shall sew your buttons on in a different place. Then you will be able to do up your jacket quite easily, I'm sure. I hope you haven't lost that middle button, Teddy Bear?'

'Oh no, Mrs Duck,' replied Teddy Bear. 'Here it is in my pocket.'

Mrs Duck sewed the buttons on one inch nearer to the edge.

'Now, Teddy Bear,' she said. 'Come and try your jacket on.'

It fitted perfectly.

'Oh, thank you, Mrs Duck,' cried Teddy Bear. 'Now I must go home – and I'll take a jar of honey with me – a large jar.'

When Teddy Bear arrived home he put the jar of honey on the table and took out a big spoon.

Then he gave a deep, growly laugh.

'Who ever heard of a *thin* bear?' he said.

Alison's new baby

Shelley R. Lee

Are you sitting comfortably? Then I'll begin.

One day Alison came downstairs to see what Mummy was doing. She wasn't in the kitchen. She wasn't in the dining room. She wasn't outside hanging out the washing. Then Alison found her. She was in the garage, with a bowl of water and a cloth, washing Alison's old pram, the one with the big wheels.

'What are you doing, Mummy?' asked Alison.

'I'm washing your old pram,' said Mummy.

'Yes,' said Alison. 'But *why* are you washing my old pram? I'm much too big to ride in it now.'

'Well,' said Mummy, 'I thought maybe we would have a new baby to put in it soon.'

So Alison helped to wash the pram, and Mummy said, 'When the new baby comes, you will be my big girl, and help to push the pram.'

Now the next day Alison came downstairs to see what Mummy was doing. She wasn't in the kitchen. She wasn't in the dining room. She wasn't outside hanging out the washing. Then Alison found her. She was in the smallest bedroom, with a bowl of water and a cloth, wiping down Alison's old baby bath.

'What are you doing, Mummy?' asked Alison.

'I'm wiping down your old baby bath,' said Mummy.

'Yes,' said Alison. 'But *why* are you wiping down my old baby bath? I'm much too big to bath in it now.'

'Well,' said Mummy, 'I thought maybe we would have a new baby to put in it soon.'

So Alison helped to wipe down the baby bath, and Mummy said, 'When the new baby comes, you will be my big girl, and help to bath the baby.'

Now the next day Alison came downstairs to see what Mummy was doing. She wasn't in the kitchen. She wasn't in the dining room. She wasn't hanging out the washing. Then Alison found her. She was looking in the chest of drawers to find Alison's old nappies.

'What are you doing, Mummy?' asked Alison.

'I'm looking for your old nappies,' said Mummy.

'Yes,' said Alison. 'But *why* are you looking for my old nappies? I'm much too big for nappies now.'

'Well,' said Mummy, 'I thought maybe we

would have a new baby to put nappies on soon.'

So Alison helped to find the nappies, and Mummy said, 'When the new baby comes, you will be my big girl and help to do the work. There is such a lot of work with new babies. You and I will manage together.'

Now the next day Alison came downstairs to see what Mummy was doing. She wasn't in the kitchen. She wasn't in the dining room. She wasn't outside hanging out the washing. Then Alison found her. She was by the front door with Daddy, putting on her coat.

'What are you doing, Mummy?' asked Alison.

'I think I will go to the hospital today,' said Mummy. 'It's time I had that new baby.'

So Alison and Daddy took Mummy to the hospital. Then Alison and Daddy came home and cooked the dinner, and washed up, and went to bed, all by themselves. They looked after each other beautifully till it was time for Mummy to bring the new baby home.

The baby was very small and very sweet. Its tiny hands and tiny fingernails could hold tightly to Alison's finger. Most of the time the baby screwed its eyes up tight and slept, but sometimes it got red in the face, and cried for milk and cuddling. It was hard work, looking after it. Everything happened just as Mummy said it would. They bathed the baby every day, and they

94

put nappies on the baby every day, and they pushed the pram every day. And every day Alison helped, because she was a big girl.

Do you know another nice thing? When Mummy and the baby came home from hospital, they brought a lovely present for Alison. It was a red telephone, and Alison was delighted with it. I'd like a red telephone, wouldn't you?

The treat

Edna Williams

Are you sitting comfortably? Then I'll begin.

'If you are good,' said Mrs Rabbit to her five children, 'You shall have a treat.'

'Hurrah,' shouted the little rabbits, as they dashed off to be good somewhere.

The smallest rabbit stayed beside his mother. He was wondering what a 'treat' was like.

'Out of my way,' said Mrs Rabbit, as she lifted a pile of dirty dishes from the table and put them into a bowl of soapy water to be washed.

'Can I have a treat?' asked the smallest rabbit.

'A treat?' cried Mrs Rabbit, forgetting for the moment what she had promised. 'A treat! Your whole life is one great treat, if you ask me.' She swished the dishes about in the soapy water.

The smallest rabbit could tell that he was going to get no treat from his busy mother, whatever it was like. He wandered into the garden, where he saw a blackbird splashing about in a pool of water.

'Do you know what a treat is like, Blackbird?' he asked.

The blackbird flew up into a tree and sang a song:

> 'See me splashing, Oh, what fun,
> Water sparkling in the sun.
> See my feathers smooth and neat,
> Bath-time is a special *treat*.'

'So that's it,' thought the smallest rabbit. He jumped into the pool and splashed about until his fur was all wet and muddy. It was fun.

'I don't call that being good,' said Mrs Rabbit, as she rubbed him dry with a rough towel. 'Now, be off with you.'

'If that is a treat,' thought the smallest rabbit, 'I don't much like it.'

He wandered further into the garden and stopped in front of a big red poppy. 'Do you know what a treat is like, Poppy?' asked the smallest rabbit.

The Poppy nodded its head and sang quietly to itself:

> 'See my petals bright and red,
> See my nodding poppy head,
> All the winter, fast asleep,
> This is such a perfect *treat*.'

'So that's it,' thought the smallest rabbit. He stood beside the poppy and nodded his head. He nodded until his neck felt stiff and tired. 'If that is a treat,' thought the smallest rabbit, 'I don't much like it.'

'Come along,' called Mrs Rabbit. 'You have all been good; we shall have our treat.'

Mrs Rabbit spread a large rug on the grass and told the five little rabbits to sit themselves down. 'On such a lovely day, we are going to have a picnic,' she said.

The little rabbits ate bran sandwiches and drank carrot wine through freshly gathered straws.

'How delicious,' thought the smallest rabbit, as he munched his way through his tenth sandwich. He thought of the blackbird, happy with his splashing. He thought of the poppy, happy with its nodding. He watched his mother and the little rabbits, happily chewing.

'A treat is anything that makes you happy,' he told himself.

He was right.

Smarticats

Anne Wellington

Are you sitting comfortably? Then I'll begin.

Smarticat had ginger fur and long white whiskers. Smarticat had big ideas. He liked to be important. He stalked about the farmyard shouting, 'Yo ho ho! I'm a bold bad pirate. Yo ho ho!'

Mrs Nobb the farmer's wife said, 'Don't be ridiculous. You look like a silly old pussy cat to me.'

Smarticat looked at his reflection in the pond, and imagined himself in pirate's clothes. Shiny black boots, baggy green trousers, a red stripey jersey, and a black patch covering one eye. And sitting on his shoulder, a parrot!

'Those are the things I must get,' said Smarticat. 'Then I'll be a pirate. Yo ho ho!'

Smarticat caught a bee and put it into a bag. Then he said, 'The first thing I want is shiny boots. Duck wears shiny boots. Yo ho ho!'

Duck was in the farmyard, splashing in a puddle.

Smarticat shouted, 'I want your shiny boots.

> I'm a bold bad pirate
> With a nasty stinging bee;
> I'll let it out to sting you
> If you don't obey me.'

Duck heard the stinging bee buzzing in the bag. So she had to give her shiny boots to Smarticat. 'My poor little feet will get wet,' she said.

Smarticat said, 'Who cares? Now I want some trousers. Scarecrow wears trousers. Yo ho ho!'

Scarecrow was flapping at the birds in the cabbage field.

Smarticat shouted, 'I want your baggy trousers.

> I'm a bold bad pirate
> With a nasty stinging bee;
> I'll let it out to sting you
> If you don't obey me.'

Scarecrow heard the stinging bee buzzing in the bag. So he had to give his trousers to Smarticat. 'My poor stick legs will get cold,' he said.

Smarticat said, 'Rubbish! Now I want a jersey. Pig wears a jersey. Yo ho ho!'

Pig was in the pigsty eating a potato.

Smarticat shouted, 'I want your stripey jersey.

> I'm a bold bad pirate
> With a nasty stinging bee;
> I'll let it out to sting you
> If you don't obey me.'

Pig heard the stinging bee buzzing in the bag. So he had to give his jersey to Smarticat. 'My poor little tummy will get chilly,' he said.

Smarticat said, 'Fiddlesticks! Now I want a black patch. Owl wears a black patch. Yo ho ho!'

Owl was in the oak tree, with both eyes closed.

Smarticat shouted, 'I want your black patch.

> I'm a bold bad pirate
> With a nasty stinging bee;
> I'll let it out to sting you
> If you don't obey me.'

Owl heard the stinging bee buzzing in the bag. So he had to give his black patch to Smarticat. 'My poor little eye can't sleep,' he said.

Smarticat said, 'Nonsense! Now I want a parrot. Mrs Nobb has a parrot. Yo ho ho!'

Smarticat went in to the farmhouse kitchen. Mrs Nobb the farmer's wife was making scones for tea, and the fat green parrot was asleep in his cage.

Smarticat shouted, "I want your fat green parrot.

I'm a bold bad pirate
With a nasty stinging bee;
I'll let it out to sting you
If you don't obey me.'

Mrs Nobb the farmer's wife said, 'Don't be ridiculous. You look like a silly old pussy cat to me. But I'll let you have my parrot if you'll let me have your bee.' Smarticat undid the cage and let the parrot out. 'Now put your bee in the cage,' said Mrs Nobb. Smarticat had big ideas, but very little brain. He didn't understand that the cage could keep a parrot in, but not a little bee that could fly between the bars.

He heard the nasty bee buzzing in the bag. 'But you needn't think you'll sting me,' he said. 'Oh no! You're going straight in your cage, little bee. Like that!'

The poor little stinging bee was very, very angry. It flew around the parrot cage twice to get its speed up. Then out it buzzed, between the bars, straight towards Smarticat. Smarticat ran faster than he'd ever run before. Into the farmyard with the stinging bee behind him!

'Help!' shouted Smarticat. 'The bee will sting my tail!'

But Duck and Scarecrow and Pig and Owl said, 'Fiddlesticks and piffle! We don't care!'

The bee chased Smarticat twice around the

farmyard till his boots fell off. And Duck put them on.

The bee chased Smarticat twice around the farmyard till his trousers fell off. And Scarecrow put them on.

The bee chased Smarticat twice around the farmyard till his jersey fell off. And Pig put it on.

The bee chased Smarticat twice around the farmyard till his patch fell off. And Owl put it on.

Then the bee chased Smarticat twice around the farmyard and out and away till they disappeared from sight.

Smarticat came back next day looking very glum. When anyone asked him if the bee had caught him up, he pretended not to hear, and looked the other way. But he did have a bandage round his tail!

The lippity loppity rabbit with the empty basket

Judith Drazin

Are you sitting comfortably? Then I'll begin.

Once upon a time, on a farm by a hill, there lived a Lippity Loppity Rabbit with an empty basket.

'Now what shall I put in my basket on this fine day?' said the rabbit to himself, and off he went, lippity loppity, to find the farmer's wife. The farmer's wife was working in the kitchen. She was rolling out the pastry to make a cheese pie for dinner.

'Please may I have something to put in my basket?' asked the rabbit, most politely.

'Certainly you may,' said the farmer's wife

kindly. 'Here is a piece of cheese and a loaf of good brown bread.'

So the rabbit put the cheese and the bread into his basket and off he went, lippity loppity, to find the farmer. The farmer was working hard in his garden, watering all his vegetables from a big can.

'Please may I have something to put in my basket?' asked the rabbit, most politely.

'Certainly you may,' said the farmer kindly. 'Here are three fresh carrots and a bunch of red radishes.'

So the rabbit put the carrots and the bunch of radishes in his basket and off he went, lippity loppity, until he came to the cherry tree. The cherry tree was in the orchard, waving her branches to and fro in the breeze.

'Please, Mrs Cherry Tree,' said the rabbit, most politely, 'may I have something to put in my basket?'

'Certainly you may,' said the cherry tree kindly. 'Here are four juicy cherries from my topmost branch.' The cherry tree shook her branches until the cherries fell to the ground, and the rabbit picked them up and put them in his basket. Then off he went, lippity loppity once more until he came to the beehive that stood by the lavender bush. The bees were making honey for their winter store.

'Please,' said the rabbit, most politely, when he saw them, 'please may I have something to put in my basket?'

'Certainly you mmmmmmay,' said the bees very kindly. 'Here is a honeycomb for you, dripping with rich honey.'

But when the Lippity Loppity Rabbit put the honeycomb carefully in his basket he had a big surprise. His basket was quite full up. 'My goodness,' he said to himself. 'I think it is time to climb to the meadow on the side of the hill and have a picnic.' So the Lippity Loppity Rabbit took his basket and climbed and climbed, nearly to the top of the hill, until he reached the meadow where the buttercups grew. Then out of his basket he took:

a piece of cheese
a loaf of brown bread
three fresh carrots
a bunch of radishes
four cherries from the topmost branch of the cherry tree
and a golden honeycomb dripping with honey.

Soon the basket was quite empty again, but the Lippity Loppity Rabbit was as full as full. 'That was the nicest picnic I have ever had,' he said to himself as he licked his sticky paws. Then he gave a great big yawn and, curling himself up in the sunshine, he fell fast asleep.

Gilbert the ostrich

Jane Holiday

Are you sitting comfortably? Then I'll begin.

The Dancer family lived in an ordinary house. Mr Dancer was ordinary. Mrs Dancer was ordinary. Martin and Donna were ordinary children. And Conker was an ordinary dog – black and white with a wagging tail. So how did they come to have an *ostrich* living with them? Nobody knew.

Anyway, the ostrich *was* living there and his name was Gilbert. Gilbert was a handsome bird with a small head, a fluffy body, long legs and big, brown eyes. He was so tall he could change all the light bulbs in the house without standing on a chair *but* he dropped them SMASH on the floor.

Everyone said what a lovely bird Gilbert was, but he had some nasty habits. He ate nuts and bolts. He ate jam jar lids. He ate the bathroom plug. He ate thirty pence left on the kitchen table. He ate the top of Donna's fountain-pen. She could still write with it, so she didn't mind. He ate the laces of Martin's football boots. Martin *did* mind. He shouted at Gilbert, 'You're a nasty, greedy bird!'

Gilbert was sad. He didn't know it was wrong to eat bootlaces.

In some ways Gilbert was very good. He drank all his milk up. Every morning, Mrs Dancer said, 'Drink all your milk, Martin,' and 'Drink your milk, Donna.' Martin and Donna always said, 'Ugh!' but Gilbert had finished every drop.

He could run very fast too. So Mrs Dancer sent him to the shops. He carried the shopping-basket on his wing. In the basket was the shopping-list and some money. Sometimes, too, he helped clean the house. He could reach up to the ceiling and dust the cobwebs away.

Everyone liked Gilbert. He was such a *polite* bird.

One afternoon Mr and Mrs Dancer took Martin and Donna to the cinema. They left Gilbert at home. Last time he went he had eaten two ashtrays. Now there was a big notice outside the cinema. It read: NO OSTRICHES.

Mrs Dancer was worried about leaving Gilbert. 'I hope he doesn't feel hungry.'

Mr Dancer was worried too. 'I hope he doesn't feel lonely.'

Martin and Donna were glad he wasn't coming. They always had to sit in the back row

108

when Gilbert came, because he was so tall.

'Be a good bird, Gilbert,' said Mrs Dancer. She left him a pint of milk and some cheese. Mr Dancer left him an old screwdriver. Martin and Donna left him some marbles.

When they came home at six o'clock, Gilbert was fast asleep in an armchair.

'He's drunk the milk,' said Mrs Dancer.

'He's eaten the cheese,' said Mr Dancer, 'and half the screwdriver.'

'And all the marbles,' said Martin and Donna.

Those weren't the only things Gilbert had eaten.

'I can't get into the bathroom,' called Martin.

'We can't get into the bedrooms,' called Mrs Dancer and Donna.

Do you know *why* they couldn't? Gilbert had eaten *all* the doorknobs. He hadn't left a single one anywhere. He'd even eaten the knob on the oven door. Mr Dancer managed to open one door with some tools. Then he opened the other doors.

They didn't have new door knobs put on though. Now all the doors in the Dancers' house are *swing* doors. You *push* them open. They *swing* to behind you. Everyone liked them better, and said that Gilbert was a good bird really.

I wonder what he will eat next. Do you?

The dragon of Penhesgyn
A traditional story
Moira Miller

Listen 'ere now and I'll tell you a story.

There was once a very fine lord and lady lived in a castle – and there was no finer castle in all of Wales. It stood at the bottom of a high mountain with a little village around it. And at the top of the mountain, in a cave, there lived a great, ugly dragon.

Now it happened one day that the fine lord and lady had a little baby son called Hugh. Oh, a fine baby he was. And nothing would do but they had to have a christening party, and invite everyone who was anyone to come to it –

including an old Welsh Wizard who was a sort of great uncle of the fine lady's.

The old wizard arrived late, all flustered and flummoxed, and went in to look at the baby.

'Dew!' he said. 'It's a fine little lad you have there. Pity about the dragon.'

'Dragon? What dragon?' asked the father.

'Big one up the mountain,' said the wizard. 'When your son's fifteen the dragon'll come down and eat him. There's horrible for you!'

'Impossible!' said the father.

'Oh, I'm not often wrong about these things, bach,' said the wizard. 'Part of my job, you know.'

And before they could ask him any more questions about the dragon, the wizard vanished in a puff of smoke.

But gradually they forgot what the wizard had said, and the years passed. Hugh grew up to be a fine little boy, and his very best friend was a boy from the village called David. His father was Jones the Smith, and he'd been born on the same day at exactly the same time as Hugh, to the very minute. So you see of course they were the best of friends. They did everything together. Played in the fields, climbed trees, fished in the river, and sometimes they climbed the mountain. But not too high, mind, because of the dragon at the top of course. And so the boys went on, playing and laughing together, until they were nearly fifteen.

On the day before his birthday Hugh's father called him in.

'I'm afraid the time has come for you to leave us, boyo,' he said. 'If you stay here much longer this terrible dragon will come looking, and who knows what'll happen? You're going for a long holiday to your Auntie Gwyneth in England. There isn't a Welsh dragon in the world would follow you there.' Before he knew properly what was happening Hugh was bundled off to Auntie Gwyneth in England.

Well, this was a sad state of affairs, and David was very upset about losing his best friend. And the more he thought about it the more angry he became. He was like that, do you see.

'Only a dragon it is,' he said, 'and dragons can be killed. I'll have a go at this one myself.'

He set off and climbed up the mountain, higher and higher. Farther than he or Hugh had ever been before. Up to where the dragon slept in his huge dark cave.

David scrambled up over the stones and boulders and at last he heard a great roaring sound. He crept up and peered round the corner of a rock, then nearly fell over with surprise. There was a great green dragon, lying sleeping in the sun, snoring and roaring something horrible. He was as big as a railway engine, I can tell you.

'Dew! It's horrible he is,' whispered David to himself. 'He'll take some killing. I'll have to think about this!'

He hurried back down the mountain again, and thought about it. He thought for days and days. And then – oh – he had a very clever idea. Listen, I'll tell you about it.

First of all he went to the castle kitchen and borrowed the biggest copper frying pan he could find. He took it home and started to polish it. He rubbed and rubbed. His father, Jones the Smith, rubbed and rubbed. His mam, Mrs Jones the Smith, rubbed and rubbed. Even the baby had a go. And at last that copper pan was just like a mirror. You could see your face in it, clear as clear.

Then David took his pan and climbed back up the mountain with it. He put it down carefully, and started to dig a great big hole, right in front of the dragon's cave. He waited till the dragon was asleep, mind; he wasn't daft, our David. And when that hole was dug, he put the pan in the bottom of it. Then he got all the people from the village to come up and watch what happened next.

He stood himself on the other side of the hole from the dragon and hurled a stone across at it.

'It's an idle great thing you are!' he shouted. 'Waken up, you horrible monster.'

The dragon turned over and grunted in his sleep, breathing out flames and smoke, and scorching all the grass around him.

David threw another rock. A bigger one this time.

'Call yourself a dragon, man!' he yelled. 'You're useless. Couldn't scare a mouse.'

The dragon woke up, thoroughly angry by this time, and roared a roar that was heard in every valley clear down to Aberystwyth. The great beast stood up and shook himself all over, and, boys, he was a *horrible* sight to behold. He roared another terrible roar and started towards David. But then he stopped at the edge of the hole.

He looked down, and there at his feet staring up at him was – what do you think? Another horrible dragon. Well that really put him out, I can tell you.

He leapt into that hole howling and roaring, and do you know, the dragon in the hole was not in the least bit frightened of him. It roared back, just as loud and just as ugly. Well that started the fight. David and the village people stood and stared. Fair amazed they were at the goings on. The roaring and howling and clouds of smoke and fire and whatnot. That dragon was going fit to bust, fighting with his own reflection in an old copper frying pan. Dragons are big, look you, but they're not very bright.

114

Well, at last it was all over. The stupid beast had fair exhausted himself, and the great clouds of smoke were just a little tiny trickle. Then David borrowed a sword and jumped down into the hole. One swipe and he'd chopped off the dragon's head. Clean as a whistle.

The people from the village were overjoyed. 'Alleluia!' they shouted, dancing back down the mountain. 'Our David's a Hero. The dragon's dead.'

So Hugh came back home again from his Auntie Gwyneth's, and he and David went fishing again, and even climbed to the very top of the mountain. They were the very best of friends all their lives after that.

And what about the Welsh Wizard? Well, I'll tell you one thing, nobody ever asked *him* to a christening again!

Angela and the custard pump
Jan Dean

Are you sitting comfortably? Then I'll begin.

Angela was cross.

She stamped her feet and made bad-tempered noises.

She marched up and down, snorting and grumbling. Oh yes, Angela was very cross.

The sun was shining and Angela wanted to be outside with it. She wanted to go to the park and throw bread to the ducks. She wanted to go to the park and play in the sand. She wanted to go to the park and whoosh down the slide.

But no, she couldn't feed the ducks, no, she couldn't make sand pies. No, she couldn't whoosh and thump. She had to stay inside and watch the custard pump!

Angela's grandmother had a shop. She made cakes and bread and biscuits. Everyone Angela knew came into grandma's shop, and they all said that Angela's grandma's cakes and bread and biscuits were the most wonderful and

116

delicious that they had ever tasted. But there was nothing, they said, nothing, nothing at all more marvellous and melting than Angela's grandma's creamy custard cupcakes. And they were right.

Some people said that Angela's grandma's creamy custard cupcakes were so amazingly mouthwatering that they must be magic. And they were right too. In the back of grandma's shop gleamed a strange machine. A fat shiny drum churned round and round, and a long silver tube stuck out into a bowl. Out of the tube and into the bowl poured the custard, a beautiful sweet stream of marvellous, magical custard.

Angela was not impressed. She didn't want to look after the pump – and she told it so. She hated the pump – and she told it so. The pump said nothing but, "Splinkety glug. Splinkety glug glug glug glug. Splinkety glug. Splinkety glug. Splinkety glug glug glug.' Which is what it always said.

Angela was so cross that she almost exploded. She raised both arms and shook both fists and her face grew redder and redder. She jumped into the air and began to shout. She howled and screeched and screamed and yelled and called the custard pump all the names she could think of!

Suddenly everything went quiet. Angela did not shout and the pump did not go, 'Splinkety glug.' Instead a huge splodge of custard squirted through the air and sprayed all over the wall. A great fat bubble of custard hiccuped from the tube and blubbered onto the floor, and an enormous bomb of custard burst from the drum and splattered all over the ceiling. Angela stood very still.

Angela's grandma came in carrying a red umbrella. She looked round the room and she looked at Angela. Angela looked at the floor. Custard dripped from the ceiling. Angela began to feel very sticky.

Angela's grandma looked at Angela for a very long time. Then she said, 'This looks like a job for the custard fairy to me. Pass me the 'phone book.'

So Angela handed her grandmother the 'phone book, and her grandmother looked under F for fairy. Then she went away to make the 'phone call.

While Angela waited for the custard fairy to arrive she began to clean up the room. She was halfway through mopping the floor when he appeared. He was a small man in blue overalls, and he popped out of the air carrying a large tool bag. On the back of his overalls MAGIC MACHINE MAINTENANCE MECHANIC was printed in glittering gold letters.

'What's this 'ere, then?' he said as he began to

fish around inside the broken pump. 'There's something very nasty in 'ere,' and out of the machine he pulled a black tangled lump.

'Well, no wonder it blew up!' he said.

'What is it?' asked Angela.

'The one thing guaranteed to stop a magic pump. Bad temper. A very large, a very ugly, very nasty piece of bad temper!'

Then he patted the pump and it set off again quite happily. 'Splinkety glug. Splinkety glug. Splinkety glug glug glug,' it went. 'Splinkety glug. Splinkety glug. Splinkety glug glug glug.'

'Shall I take this with me, or do you want it back?' He held the black lump out to Angela.

'No, you take it,' Angela said. 'I feel better without it.'

'Righto, then,' smiled the maintenance fairy, 'I'll be off down the road. Seems there's a pump down there running lumpy.' And he disappeared with a sort of 'ping'.

'I'm sorry, custard pump,' said Angela. 'I do like you really.'

'Splinkety glug,' said the pump. 'Splinkety glug. Splinkety glug glug glug,' and blew her a big custardy kiss.

Amy Kate's lion

Joyce Williams

Are you sitting comfortably? Then I'll begin.

It was a windy day. Amy Kate was looking for a lion. She marched along the street with a butterfly net over her shoulder, and her friends all asked, 'How are you going to catch him, Amy Kate?'

'With my butterfly net,' Amy Kate replied. 'That's what it's for.'

'What will you do with him when you've got him?'

'I shall take him to the zoo,' said Amy Kate. 'That's where all the lions belong.'

120

'Won't he be very fierce and frighten everyone?' they asked.

'I shall talk to him gently while I tie a bit of string to his collar – then he'll be quite tame,' Amy Kate assured them. 'There's no need for anyone to be frightened.'

'*I'm* frightened!' said the littlest child, but nobody heard her.

All her friends got into a long line behind Amy Kate and followed her along the street. 'Amy Kate's looking for a lion!' they told all the people. 'And we're helping her!'

'*I'm* not!' said the littlest child.

On and on they went. The wind smacked their cheeks and tugged their hair and snatched all their breaths away. Amy Kate's friends began to get tired. 'Where's this lion, Amy Kate?' they said. 'We don't believe there *is* one after all.'

'Yes, there is,' said Amy Kate. And just then a Big Brown Something came rushing out of nowhere along the street towards them. 'Here he comes!' cried Amy Kate. 'Don't be frightened!'

But the children *were* frightened. They scrambled over the wall into old Mrs Toppett's garden.

'Mrs Toppett, Mrs Toppett, there's a lion in the road and Amy Kate is chasing him!' they shouted.

The old lady came out of her cottage. 'Dear me! A lion! Has it escaped from the zoo?' Then she saw the Big Brown Something rushing along with Amy Kate after it.

Mr Podger came out of his house next door. Mrs Toppett called to him, 'Oh, Mr Podger! A lion has escaped from the zoo and Amy Kate is chasing him!'

'Goodness me!' said Mr Podger. He put on his spectacles and peered along the road. He saw a Big Brown Something going very fast, and Amy Kate racing after it, brandishing her butterfly net. Suddenly they both turned a corner and disappeared.

Policeman Blackie came by. Mr Podger, Mrs Toppett and all the children clustered round him. 'Policeman Blackie!' they shouted all together. 'A lion has escaped from the zoo and Amy Kate has chased it around a corner!'

'Hmm,' said the policeman. 'This calls for an investigation.' He strode off down the street with big heavy steps. Mr Podger trotted after him. Mrs Toppett hurried after Mr Podger. Behind her came all the children in a straggly line, the littlest child last of all clinging to her brother.

At the corner Policeman Blackie stopped, and Mr Podger, Mrs Toppett and all the children bumped into one another as they stopped too. They peeped around the corner. There, partly hidden behind a dustbin, was the Big Brown Something, but Amy Kate was nowhere to be seen.

'The lion must have eaten her!' the littlest child whispered.

Suddenly the Big Brown Something sprang out at them from behind the dustbin, and everybody screamed.

'Why, it's only a large paper bag after all!' said Policeman Blackie. 'The wind must have blown it along.' He began to laugh.

'Just fancy that!' declared Mrs Toppett and Mr Podger. 'A brown paper bag!' They went off home looking rather disappointed.

'But where is Amy Kate?' demanded all the children.

Just then Amy Kate bobbed up from behind the dustbin, and began to whistle in an offhand manner. She shouldered her butterfly net and strolled towards them.

'Amy Kate, Amy Kate, where's the lion?' chanted the children.

'Gone,' said Amy Kate.

'Back to the zoo?'

Amy Kate shook her head. 'He begged me not to send him to the zoo. He said his home was in Africa, so I made him promise to go there straight away. And that's what he did.'

'What are you doing now, Amy Kate?' they asked.

'Me? I'm looking for an elephant,' replied

Amy Kate. 'Want to come along?'

'Will he bite?' asked the littlest child.

'Of course not,' said Amy Kate. 'He'll give us rides on his back.'

'Hurrah!' cried all the children. 'We're looking for an elephant!' They got into a line behind Amy Kate. Then they all went whistling down the street.

All it needs is a wash

Armorel Kay Walling

Are you sitting comfortably? Then I'll begin.

Tina went to a jumble sale with her Mum – and bought a hat. Not a hat for herself, not a hat for her doll, but a hat for her big brother Bob.

Bob was at a football match. Bob loved watching football. He always wore something blue and white when he went to a football match because those were the colours of his favourite team. The hat Tina bought was blue and white, too: blue and white stripes with a big blue bobble on top.

'Bob can wear it to football,' said Tina, 'to keep his ears warm.'

'It's grubby,' said Mum.

'It's beautiful,' said the jumble sale lady. 'All it needs is a wash.'

So as soon as she got home, Tina washed the hat. She stood on a chair at the sink and shook soap powder into the bowl. She turned on the taps and woggled the water in the bowl until it was dancing with bubbles. Then she turned them off again and began to scrub. She rubbed and scrubbed. She scrubbed and rubbed for so long that her hands became all crinkly from being in the water, and she used most of the soap powder. But the hat – why the hat came out as clean as new!

'There!' said Tina. 'I *knew* all it needed was a wash!'

She went outside, let down the line, and pegged the hat out to dry.

Then she sat down with Mum for a drink and a biscuit. (It was a chocolate biscuit – rather sticky.) After a while, she thought, 'I wonder if that hat's dry yet?' and went to look.

It wasn't, of course, so she decided to help *blow* it dry. She stood very close and pursed her lips and went 'Foooo!' Sadly, she still had chocolate on her lips, and when she went 'Fooo!' some of it came off and left a smudge on the hat.

'Never mind,' thought Tina, 'it's only a little smudge,' and she went indoors to paint pictures.

But after a while she thought, 'I wonder if it's dry *now*,' and went to look.

It wasn't, of course, so she tried to *squeeeeeze* it dry. Sadly, her hands were still pink from painting, and when she squeezed some of the pink came off on the hat and made a stain.

'Never mind,' thought Tina, 'it's only a little

stain,' and she went to watch television.

But after a while, she thought, 'I wonder if it's dry *yet*,' and went to have another look. It *still* wasn't, so very carefully she took the hat off the line and laid it on her swing. She decided to push it high into the sky so that the winter sun could dry it. Sadly, the hat flew off and fell – right into the cabbages. They left a muddy streak.

'Oh dear,' thought Tina. 'It's quite a big streak.'

Suddenly, she heard Bob coming home from football. She didn't want him to see the hat – not until it was dry – so she ran indoors and pushed it quickly down behind the radiator. And then, what with Bob being excited because his favourite team had won, and there being apple crumble for supper, Tina forgot about the hat – until next day.

How proud she was when she remembered that she'd washed it all by herself. She pulled it out from behind the radiator. It was rather dusty, and it *did* still have a chocolate smudge and a pink paint stain and a muddy cabbage streak but – now it was *dry*.

She gave it to Bob.

'What's this?' he asked gruffly.

'A present for you. I bought it with my own money – to keep your ears warm at football.'

Bob looked at the hat slowly; at the chocolate

smudge and the pink paint stain and the muddy streak and the dusty patch, and for a moment Tina thought he didn't like it.

Then he smiled. 'Thank you,' he said. 'Thank you, Tina. It's a beautiful hat and it *will* keep my ears warm at football. There's just one thing... it's grubby.'

'Oh *that*,' said Tina. 'Don't worry about *that*. All it needs is a wash!' And off she skipped to get the soap powder again.